Lucy & the Lake Monster

By
Richard Rossi
& Kelly Tabor

Volume One, First Edition

Soon To Be A Major Motion Picture

Eternal Grace Publishing
Hollywood, California

Copyright © 2022 Richard Rossi & Kelly Tabor

Eternal Grace Publishing   N. Hollywood, California

Lucy & the Lake Monster

Volume One, First Edition

All Rights Reserved

No part of this publication may be reproduced, distributed, or transmitted in any form or by any means, including photocopying, recording, or other electronic or mechanical methods, without the prior written permission of the publisher, except in the case of brief quotations embodied in critical reviews and certain other non-commercial uses permitted by copyright law.

This book is a work of fiction. Any references to historical events, real people, or real places are used fictitiously. Other names, characters, places and events are products of the author's imagination, and any resemblance to actual events, places or persons, living or dead, is entirely coincidental.

Facebook.com/ChampMovie

@ChampMovieHQ on Twitter and Instagram

Printed in the United States of America

First Printing, 2022

First Edition, 2022

"Canst thou draw out leviathan with a hook?
Or his tongue with a cord which thou lettest down?

Out of his mouth goeth burning lamps,
and sparks of fire leap out.

Out of his nostrils goeth smoke,
as out of a seething pot or caldron.

His breath kindleth coals,
and a flame goeth out of his mouth."

Job 41:1, 19-21

Table of Contents

Chapter 1 Mama's Gone...1

Chapter 2 Heaven...11

Chapter 3 Dreams..19

Chapter 4 A Trip to Town 27

Chapter 5 Signs and Wonders...39

Chapter 6 Captain Blye's...45

Chapter 7 Lago Time..55

Chapter 8 Looking for Champ...61

Chapter 9 Camera Ready...71

Chapter 10 Bullies..83

Chapter 11 God Don't Make Junk...87

Chapter 12 Legacy..93

Chapter 13 Take A Picture!..101

Chapter 14 Naysayers...107

Chapter 15 Bad Guys...117

Chapter 16 Birthday 125

Chapter 17 Baptism 133

Chapter 18 Champ Chomp Chum 139

Chapter 19 Shocking Sight 149

Chapter 20 A Dream Come True..157

Chapter 21 Hometown Heroes 169

Chapter 22 Magic and Love...181

About The Authors..189

Also by Richard Rossi 190

Chapter 1
Mama's Gone

It was just before Lucy Lago's bedtime on a late spring evening and she tended to think of big things at night. Her eyebrows crinkled as she thought as hard as she could, trying to figure out where her mother went. She looked down to the dirty floor of Papa's rustic cabin with a blank stare.

Papa built a fireplace for heat and dug a well for fresh running water from the spring. He put in a septic tank for plumbing. The cabin had a small kitchen area with a gas refrigerator and stove. Papa built a table, which was underneath a picture window that overlooked the lake. There were modest furnishings Papa had made with his hands: a dresser, a cabinet for dishes, two beds, and two chairs. Lucy sat on one and Papa sat on the other. Underneath Papa's bed was the newspaper.

Papa loved the luxury of receiving the weekly free edition and reading it cover-to-cover. He liked the feeling of holding the newspaper in his hands, and his favorite section was Sports. He read the baseball scores and recalled when he played second base on his school team, alongside future Major League pitcher Johnny Podres. Podres was the only person to become famous from Lucy's hometown area and a giant sign of Podres in his Dodgers uniform commemorated this on Main Street.

1

Lucy & the Lake Monster

Even though she was just nine years-old, Lucy Lago had a big bunch of courage. She was a gutsy girl, with more determination than any adult in her town of two-thousand people, Crown Point, New York, located in Essex County. Crown Point was on the west shore of Lake Champlain, a stone's throw from the Vermont border. Lucy had been surrounded by Lake Champlain ever since she was born.

During the American Revolution, Crown Point was a strategic location, the northernmost fort under American control. Papa's log cabin was a fort for Lucy, a strong, secure base in the battle against mockery and mercenary forces opposing their search for a sea serpent named Champ.

Papa, sixty, rocked back and forth in his chair. He had built every inch of the sunbaked cabin on the lake, cutting down the pine trees and laying the logs. Some of the clay between the logs had dried and crumbled recently. Papa had worked into the dark, chinking the cabin with new mud and pebbles between the logs, to keep the north wind out and the cabin trim, safe, and secure for little Lucy. Whenever he looked at Lucy, his eyes grew warmer and brighter.

"Where's Mama?" Lucy asked her grandpa, who she called "Papa," or "Papa Jerry."

"Heaven. She's with the angels, honey," Papa said, gazing out at Lake Champlain and the Adirondack Mountains.

Papa's blue eyes were the same color as the sea. They were the one thing about his face that remained young, in contrast to his silver beard and the brown bumps elevated on the right side of his face. He caught sight of Bulwagga Mountain, one of the Adirondacks nearest them that stood one thousand four hundred twenty-seven feet. Papa exhaled deeply, his breath draining out as he thought about how Bulwagga Mountain drained its winter snow. Its tributaries leaked into the lake to raise the water level.

"Is she just with angels, or is she with any people, Papa?" Lucy asked.

"Your Mama's with your Daddy, who died in a war a long time ago, just before you were born."

Lucy's big, blue eyes looked to the brown wall of the cabin where three pictures hung: her mother Lynn, her father Gary in military uniform, and a picture of the Sacred Heart of Jesus. Then, her eyes glanced up to the roof of their dusty log cabin that sat on the rocky shoreline of Lake Champlain. She imagined Mama and Daddy looking over her. She made circles with her fingers and put them over her eyes, like the binoculars her and Papa used when they went out on Lake Champlain in their wooden rowboat. Her mouth wrinkled a bit trying to imagine Heaven.

Lucy was quiet for a few moments, remembering her mother's accident. Though it was two years prior, when she was just seven, Lucy still remembered seeing the swirling police lights and hearing the distress calls on the police radios. She smelled a mixture of gas from the boat and her mother's perfume and wondered if she was dreaming it all. Ever since that tragic night, Lucy felt panic creeping up from the basement of her mind and a bitter, metallic taste in her mouth whenever she saw cop cars. The accident was a distant memory now, like a nightmare fading in the morning light.

Her Papa Jerry's strong hand held her little hand and led her safely back to his cabin on the lake that tragic night. She remembered the howl of the wind and the Adirondack coyotes as she stumbled on Papa's battered fishing creel when they entered the cabin. Ever since then, Papa put the fishing creel in the corner of the cabin, away from the door.

Papa wanted to find Champ now too, and though his cabin was humble, he made it a home for Lucy, a place where they could heal and look for Champ together.

Lucy petted Bella, her tri-colored Yorkshire Terrier with a silky coat of grey, tan, and white fur. She and Bella cuddled.

She noticed the stripes on her blue shirt were horizontal, and the stripes on Papa's red flannel went up and down. Despite this difference, she liked imitating Papa and wore blue jean overalls like him. She tied a blue ribbon in her hair to match her shirt and pants.

Lucy liked the color blue because it matched the color of her and Papa's eyes. "Blue is the color of my eyes, and the eyes of my Lucy," Papa said. "The color of the sky, and the color of the sea."

Lucy would answer. "Blue is the color of the eyes of Papa and me. The color of the sky, and the color of the sea." This was something she and Papa said whenever they saw something blue.

Lucy knew there was magic and love waiting for her in the lake. She looked out the window towards the direction of the four-hundred-foot-long Lake Champlain Bridge that connected New York to Vermont with its triangle trusses. She wondered what bridge connected this world to the next, Heaven to Earth.

Lucy sighed, breathing out a deep breath the way Papa did a moment earlier. She didn't remember her father at all, but she had a picture of him in his army ASU dress blues uniform. Her late father had big brown eyes and such perfect features, he looked like a mannequin.

4

Papa always flew a big American flag from their cabin in honor of Lucy's father. Papa's favorite fisherman's hat had a flag on it, too.

Lucy had wonderful memories of her mother Lynn, who used to sing to her and tell her stories about Champ. Sometimes she had dreams of her mother, surrounded by mist and light, looking peaceful.

"I'm proud of you, Lucy," her mother told her in her dreams. "Proud of your efforts to find Champ."

Champ was known as "America's Loch Ness," because a similar sea serpent named Nessie was spotted in a lake in Loch Ness, Scotland.

"I get tired of them calling Champ 'America's Loch Ness,'" her mother Lynn had once told her. "I'm so proud of Champ that I think he's better than Nessie. We should reverse it, and call Nessie 'Scotland's Champ.'" Lynn and Lucy chuckled.

"Yes, Mommy," Lucy said, "because Champ *is* much more special to us."

Her Mama had a contagious smile, with sparkling teeth that made others smile back. Lucy remembered this, then looked at Papa's face and saw the same smile. Her mother was Papa's daughter.

"Champ is from another world," Lucy's mother had told her in one of her stories. "He's magical. Our best friend. He has a strong grip when you ride him and he can take us to another world."

"Papa?" Lucy asked, thinking of the world to come as she remembered her mother's stories.

Lucy & the Lake Monster

"Yes, Lucy?"

"How do we know that Heaven's real and Mama is still alive?" Lucy asked, moving her hands as she talked the way Papa did sometimes. "How do we know it's not made up?" She crossed her arms like she was hugging and holding herself.

(This thought made her voice crack with a squeaky sound, because *If Heaven wasn't real,* she thought, *I'll never see Mama again.*)

Papa froze for a second, unsure what to say. He felt like a white-tailed deer caught in the crossbows of a Lake Champlain hunter, because the same question had haunted and hunted him. The memory of his daughter Lynn's accident flooded back again to him.

Thirty-three-year-old Lynn Lago's Bayliner Bowrider boat was sucked into the waters of Lake Champlain as the hungry hands of the lake pulled her down. She'd been searching for the sea serpent Champ, who was rumored to live in the lake that borders New York and Vermont.

Papa Jerry was nervous, with an almost animal awareness of the impending storm. He had warned Lynn that there was a bad Nor'easter creeping down from Canada that day, but Lynn was determined to find Champ, despite the wicked winds and wild waves on the lake. The towns of Crown Point and Port Henry quivered under the assault of the mighty winds. Jerry never forgot her haunting last words.

"I'm in God's hands, Daddy," Lynn had said.

"That's what I'm afraid of," Papa Jerry Lago replied.

After the accident, Jerry was angry for a while.

First, he was angry at Champ and even at God, blaming the sea serpent story and reckless faith for his daughter's death.

The legend of the lake was that Champ was once a great Indian brave. He was spurned by his lover, Bulwagga, the Indian princess. Then, he flew into a jealous rage when he learned she'd chosen another suitor over him. He pushed Bulwagga and she fell deep into the depths of Lake Champlain and drowned. He wanted to die with the love of his life, so he tied rocks around his legs and jumped into the lake where he was magically transformed into the sea monster Champ. Papa knew it was a legend, but he sometimes wondered if Champ had drowned Lynn, just like he'd drowned Bulwagga. The bay where she drowned was now named after the Indian princess.

Papa Jerry was not just angry at Champ and God. He was angry at Lynn for going out on the lake against his warnings. Then, he felt guilty for feeling furious at her for dying every time he looked out at the crypt-still spot on the lake where she went down.

Lake Champlain, once a crystal-clear mirror reflecting sunny skies, was now polluted by bad memories for Jerry Lago. Like the zebra mussels that invaded the lake, multiplying and changing the ecosystem, scratching swimmers and filtering algae, his view of the lake was tainted by his grief.

Lastly, he felt angry at himself for not doing more to stop Lynn from venturing out in the storm. His anger subsided with the realization that his granddaughter Lucy needed the best of his love. He had to hide his pain from her, so he didn't pollute her pure soul the way the zebra mussels polluted the lake.

Lucy determined to complete her mother's mission and find Champ. Champ was not a monster to Lucy, even though what happened to her mother was monstrous. Lucy believed in Champ, the legend of the lake.

Papa did not want Lucy in the court system as an orphan looking for a foster home. He wanted to take care of her himself. After all, she was his flesh and blood. Lucy lived with Papa since Mama's boating accident.

"How do we know that Heaven's real and Mama's still alive?" Lucy asked again, repeating her question and jarring Papa back to the present.

Papa recovered his composure to answer Lucy. "You believe in Champ even though others don't," Papa said.

"Yes, but I still have questions, Papa."

He took off his fisherman's cap for a moment to scratch his salt-and-pepper hair. Papa was never irritated with Lucy's questions. This made him the opposite of some impatient adults who Lucy had encountered in the past. "Your questions are the sign of your intelligence, Lucy," Papa said.

"If Mama died looking for Champ, he must be real," Lucy said.

"There are things that are real we don't always see, Lucy," Papa said. "Your Mama's body is still here, somewhere in the lake, but she's not actually gone. There are some very strange things in that lake, very strange. Lake Champlain has been around a long time. There are secrets behind it's wrinkled face, and it does not give up its secrets easily."

Papa paused, thinking about how only fragments of the outboard boat wreckage were located, but no trace of Lucy's mother. It was still a mystery, just like the prehistoric plesiosaur Champ was one of the mysteries of science.

Thoughts of the accident invaded Lucy, too, like the round goby fish invaded Lake Champlain. The goby was a nest robber, from cargo ships. They came from the Black Sea to feed on the eggs of other species in the bottom of the lake. Lucy's grief came up, unexpectedly sometimes, from the Black Sea of her memory, to haunt the fragile shell of her mind.

"Will we see Mama again?" Lucy asked, repeating the question she asked many times.

"The part of your Mama that lives on isn't a part of the body doctors take care of. It's the invisible soul," Papa said. "The part that feels love and happiness. Most people throughout the world believe that part lives on, so we can believe we'll see her again."

Lucy's face turned happy at the thought of seeing Mama again. She snuggled with Bella under her soft, fluffy, blue blanket.

"There is no reason to think it isn't true," Papa said.

Lucy felt comforted and remembered her mother's smiling face singing a song to her she had written.

Heaven is awaiting me

And I can't wait to finally see

The legend of the lake face to face

Chapter 2
Heaven

"What do you think Heaven looks like, Lucy?" Papa asked as he sat in his rocker and doodled some notes on his beat-up guitar.

Lucy rubbed her chin. "Hmmmm..." she said, thinking to herself at first. She had a creative mind, and smiled as she imagined what Heaven might be like. She remembered some of her mother's stories of Heaven.

"I think Heaven has cotton-candy clouds," Lucy said. "They're puffy and fluffy. Heaven's a beautiful place. It's always a bright sky. Like a shiny, sunny day at the beach. The seagulls feed from our hands. Angels also live there, with birds and butterflies, and all the people who died."

"Can you imagine your Mama living there?"

"Well..." (Lucy had a habit of saying "hmmmm" or "well" when she thought about things and started putting her words together). "I picture Mama living in one of the cloud castles. Her driveway is made of gold. Her house has a rainbow roof and her yard is a meadow with the greenest grass under the clearest blue sky. Oh, and she has a pet unicorn."

At the mention of a pet, Lucy's little Yorkie Bella barked and her ears stood to attention.

"Animals we love will be there and Bella will be there, too." She petted Bella. "They cross the Rainbow Bridge, just this side of Heaven, to join us. White horses will be there, like it says in the last book of the Bible. Champ will be there one day, too."

Lucy & the Lake Monster

Papa marveled at Lucy's love for Champ, despite the traumatic memory that her mother died looking for him. He knew he had to have the courage to believe in the goodness Lucy believed in, and not let his pain over Lynn's accident define his view of Champ. Deep down though, his soul felt murky like the waters of the clay-bottom Lake Champlain.

Lucy's remarks about horses triggered his memories. He remembered when he was a boy, he earned candy money caring for horses that were boarded in a barn in Port Henry. He shoveled manure, groomed, and fed the horses.

One day, he was tempted to hop on a wild horse. The farmers named the feral horse "Nuckalavee," which meant "demon horse" that roamed the fields. Despite the farmers warnings to never ride Nuckalavee, Jerry rode the tan mustang bareback and was thrown far, landing in the weeds, unconscious.

He recovered in the hospital, missing months of school. He'd slowly recovered his strength and courage to care for horses again, but there was a nagging fear of feral horses in the back of his mind.

Papa looked at Lucy, realizing his ambivalent feelings towards Champ were the same as his boyhood feelings about horses. He would support Lucy's quest to find Champ, despite his doubts, choosing to focus on whatsoever was pure and good in his granddaughter's faith. His mind returned to the present, thinking of something else to ask Lucy about Heaven.

"What does Heaven smell like, Lucy?" Papa asked, scratching his trim silver beard.

"Hmmmm. Well...we breathe in fields of fragrant flowers like roses, lavenders, and lily of the valleys. Even though we walk through them, they are never flattened from our feet. Every step we take makes us happier because of its satisfying smell."

"What else do you smell, Lucy?"

"Chocolate chip cookies fresh out of the oven, when they're gooey and good."

"Do we eat the cookies, Lucy?" Papa asked.

Lucy's face crinkled. "If Heaven is a place where everyone is satisfied and peaceful, then why would we get hungry there, Papa?" Lucy inquired.

Other kids in her class sometimes laughed at her questions. Her friend Ricky Taschner's mother said she asked too many questions, and some of them were inappropriate. A few weeks earlier, Mrs. Taschner had Lucy as a student in her Sunday School at Pastor Crowder's church in Port Henry. Ricky's mom was teaching from the beginning of Genesis, the story of the creation of the world.

Lucy kept raising her hand asking rapid-fire questions. "Mrs. Taschner you said the world is proof of God because if something exists, someone had to have created it. My question is, if God exists, who created God?"

"Uh, er," Mrs. Taschner stammered, not sure how to answer. "Lucy please don't interrupt with questions during lesson time."

"Okay, Mrs. Taschner," Lucy had said. "I promise to listen and not ask any more questions."

A few minutes later, Mrs. Taschner talked about the devil coming as a serpent in the Garden of Eden.

Lucy & the Lake Monster

Lucy broke her promise to be quiet and asked, "If God knows everything, he knew the serpent was bad, so why wouldn't he protect his children Adam and Eve, the way Papa protects me and keeps me safe. Papa keeps me away from bad people, why didn't God keep the devil away from Adam and Eve?"

Mrs. Taschner, couldn't answer this question either, so she kicked Lucy out of church and sent her home to Papa. From that moment on, her son, Ricky Taschner, thought Lucy was too cool for Sunday School and had a humungous crush on her.

Lucy cried after being kicked out of church because she wanted Pastor Crowder, the minister at the church, to baptize her. After Mrs. Taschner shamed her for her questions, Lucy thought to herself, *If I ever get baptized, it will be somewhere other than the church building.*

Lucy couldn't stop her questions about God and Heaven from coming to her mind since her mother's accident.

"If Heaven is a place where everyone is satisfied and peaceful, then why would we get hungry there, Papa?" Lucy repeated, because her voice was soft when she asked the first time and Papa hadn't heard her.

"The Bible does talk about a supper in Heaven," Papa said.

"Yes, but if there's no death in Heaven, animals or plants won't die for us to eat them, Papa. Besides, when we eat, we go to the bathroom, and that would smell yucky, and there's no yuckiness in Heaven."

"I never thought of that," Papa said. "You amaze me with your questions, Lucy."

"Well, if the Bible says there's a supper, maybe we eat, Papa. There are trees there that have a different fruit to eat every month of the year. Twelve different delicious fruits. Better than any we've tasted on earth.

"What would you like to eat in Heaven, Lucy?"

"Treats, like chocolate and other surprises. Maybe the angels serve us treats on golden platters."

"You're making me hungry for a bedtime snack," Papa said, smiling. "What does Heaven *sound* like?"

"We will hear the sweetest songs," Lucy said. "You know how you tap your foot and count when you strum your guitar, Papa?"

"Yes," Papa said. Papa strummed a few chords. "One, two, three, four," Papa counted, tapping his foot.

The guitar had a gash in it, and was beat-up like their cabin, but Papa could make it sing.

"Well, in Heaven, we time travel so the music has the best beat ever," Lucy said. "It's a timing beyond one-two-three-fours. The songs are sung by angels, with magic words that aren't found in the dictionary," Lucy said.

"What do you think people are like in Heaven?"

"Everyone loves each other. There are no bullies or mean people, like the kids at school who make fun of me for believing in Champ. Mama's neighbors are nice. No one gets sick, tired, or dies. In the cotton-candy cloud castles, there are cotton beds more comfortable to rest on than any bed on earth."

"What do you think it will be like when we get there, Lucy?"

"It's gonna be like a family reunion when we get there. We'll see all the family, friends, and pets who passed away. So, we'll meet family we never met before that lived long before we were here."

"I lost my mother when I was young," Papa said. "She died giving birth to my youngest sister. Both our mothers are together now."

"It's a perfect paradise. It's so wonderful, Papa."

"That sounds wonderful," Papa said, nodding. "Speaking of cotton candy beds, it's past your bedtime, Lucy."

"I know," Lucy said in a whiny tone.

After brushing her teeth and saying her bedtime prayers, Papa tucked Lucy into her pine bed, then fed her a bedtime snack, apple slices and chocolate milk. He made a funny face to make her laugh and forget she was upset about going to bed. If she had her way, however, she would stay up past her bedtime every night.

"Papa?"

"Yes, Lucy?"

"Even though Heaven is a wonderful place, I don't want Mama in Heaven. I want her here with me."

"I know, Lucy. Me too," Papa said.

Papa gave Lucy a kiss goodnight on her forehead, then pulled the covers over her tightly. Lucy heard the sound of the rain on the roof of the snug cabin. Bella snored beside her. The crickets and cicadas were loud enough to keep her up for a while, but then she started to fade. She looked towards the window as the first dark clouds of nightfall came. In the hush of night, the moon's light lanced Lucy's blinds. Silver shadows danced across her wall. She laid back in bed and the last thing she saw was Papa's handmade cane fishing poles in the rafters of the cabin.

Soon Lucy was drifting into dreamland, dreaming of Champ. Little did she know, her greatest adventures with Champ were just around the corner.

Chapter 3
Dreams

The loud rumble of distant thunder shook their cabin. Flashes of lightning lit the lake and lifted Lucy out of her dream.

"Champ!" Lucy yelled so loud she woke up Papa, who rushed in to check on her.

Papa was used to nighttime outbursts because Lucy had dreams that seemed so real, she often woke up breathing fast and sweating. Outside, it was still dark and drizzling. The Monday morning dawn was still a couple hours away.

"Are you okay, sweetie?" Papa asked, sitting on her bed and wiping her wet forehead with a tissue.

"Yes, Papa."

"Were you dreaming again?"

"All my life I wanted to see him. I keep having dreams about Champ." Lucy's grin let Papa know it wasn't a nightmare, but a delightful dream.

"What does Champ do in your dreams?" Papa asked.

Lucy did what Papa called her "Lucy look" which was her looking up and to the side as she thought deeply. Lucy knew dreams can slip away from her memory if she didn't talk about them right away. She closed her eyes and squinted to bring the dream back in her mind, like watching a movie.

Lucy & the Lake Monster

"Champ comes up to me on to the rocks in front of our cabin and talks to me," Lucy said, folding her hands together. "On the spot where we fish for sunfish, perch, and sheepsheads."

"What does he look like, Lucy?"

"Champ looks like a long-necked dinosaur. He's always friendly." She smiled a friendly smile, remembering. "He's never someone to be afraid of."

Lucy thought of Champ as her friend, not a horrible lake monster. She felt Champ's love wrapping around her like her fuzzy blue blanket.

At first, Papa thought Lucy might fear Champ, because her mother died looking for him. Papa was glad Lucy retained her happy feelings and banished the bad ones, but he wanted to always be there when Lucy looked for Champ, to prevent tragedy striking twice.

"What happened next in your dream, Lucy?" Papa asked.

"Champ let me ride him," Lucy said. Then, Champ breathed fire that turned into cotton candy hearts of different colors that circled around my neck."

"Was I in the dream?" Papa asked.

"Yes, Papa. We sang, 'You, Champ, and Me' which made Champ so happy he tooted colors out of his mouth and ears." ('You, Champ, and Me,' was a special song Lucy and Papa wrote some lyrics to together. Lucy, like her mother Lynn before her, wrote songs with Papa).

"How exciting," Papa said, strumming a G chord and singing the song. "My sweet Lucy, on our boat upon the sea..."

Lucy joined in. "Just you, Champ, and me," Lucy sang with her fresh, innocent voice.

"Can we go down to the lake and look for Champ today, Papa?"

"Yes, but it's easier to find someone if you know what you're looking for. What did his skin look like, Lucy?"

"Well, his skin was the color of a green garbage bag." This made Lucy chuckle. "It's hard, like a turtle shell." She did her "Lucy look" again, gazing to her upper right for a moment.

"I saw him for a couple minutes. He has a smiling face and a head shaped like a chicken nugget," Lucy continued. "He likes to bounce and bop up and down." She bounced in her bed as she said this. "He has small flippers that sometimes stick up out of the water as he swims." She made a high whistling sound as she moved her arms like flippers. This made Papa smile.

"That's what Champ looked like when I saw him years ago," Papa said. "I was fishing for pike when I saw two humps come out of the water, gliding like a submarine. His skin was green, like you said, and he slithered through the lake like a snake. He had a long neck, and his head was similar to a horse's head."

"Have others seen him too, Papa?"

"Yes, others have seen Champ too, Lucy. There are over three hundred eyewitnesses. Some of their names are on the sign in Bulwagga Bay with the sighting dates."

"Can we see the sign today and the names?"

"Sure, Lucy."

"Has Champ been seen for a long time, Papa?"

Lucy & the Lake Monster

"The Abenaki Indians saw him thousands of years ago. They called him "Gitaskog." The famous French explorer, Samuel de Champlain also saw him." Papa walked over to his dusty bookshelf and pulled out a book about Champlain.

"Lake Champlain was named after him, and Champ got his name from shortening "Champlain" to "Champ." He mapped the lake on the way to Canada. He wrote about seeing Champ. He even drew him in his journal. He was the first to see him in July of 1609. Here are some of his drawings."

Lucy looked at Champ's horse-shaped head and snaky, strong neck in the sketches. "That's him! That's what I saw in my dream, Papa!"

"Here's how he described Champ in his own words," Papa said. He pointed to Champlain's words and read aloud. "He was a twenty-foot serpent as thick as a barrel with a head like a horse.' These drawings are hundreds of years ago."

Papa and Lucy paged through the pencil drawings from the 1600's of Champ by Samuel de Champlain and Native Americans. Lucy marveled at Champ's long neck and humungous body in the sketches. The paper was aged and yellow but the drawings seemed to be alive. Lucy half-expected the Champ drawings to move, like animated cartoons.

"That would make Champ very old, Papa."

"Yes, either Champ lives a long time, or there may be more than one. A family of Champs that continue to have baby Champs. Perhaps the Champ we'll see when we explore is a descendant of the Champ in these drawings, like you are a descendant of me."

"Baby Champs?" Lucy said.

Lucy picked up a green dinosaur Champ toy on her nightstand. Papa bought it for her at Champ's Trading Post, just across the border in Addison, Vermont. She played with her Champ toy, dipping it up and down. She pursed and puckered her lips and made the Champ high whistling sound again. Bella answered the sound with her high-pitched bark.

"Do you have babies, Champ?" Lucy said to her toy.

"Yes, I do," Lucy answered back in a low voice and friendly growl, pretending she was Champ, then did the Champ whistling in the water sound.

"Are there any books that describe Champ that are even older than the 1600's?" Lucy asked.

"Yes, one of the oldest books, the Book of Job, describes a creature like what we saw. The Good Lord made all creatures, big and small."

"Some other people don't believe in you Champ, like Papa and I do," Lucy said to her green dinosaur toy. "We know you're real."

Papa took his old Bible off the shelf and read from the Book of Job. It was a long poem with the words in the center of the page:

Can you pull in the mighty sea serpent with a fishhook
or tie down its tongue with a rope?
Can you put a cord through his nose?

Lucy listened, really paying attention as Papa continued:

I will not fail to speak of the sea serpent's limbs,
its strength and its graceful form.
Who can strip off its outer coat?

23

Lucy & the Lake Monster

Who can penetrate its double coat of armor?
Who dares open the doors of its mouth?
Its back has rows of shields
tightly sealed together;
each is so close to the next
that no air can pass between.
They are joined fast to one another;
they cling together and cannot be parted.
Its eyes are like the rays of dawn.
and flames dart from its mouth.
Strength resides in its neck;
Its chest is hard as rock,
hard as a lower millstone.
Nothing on earth is its equal—
a creature without fear.
It is king over all that are proud.

"That's my Champ!" Lucy said with a big smile.

"Your Mama believed in Champ, too," Papa said.

"Tell me about her, Papa?"

"I see her in you. You're so much like her. When I'm with you, I feel her with us," Papa said. He fought back the tears that were starting to cloud his eyes.

"Mama's in Heaven, but I still have you, Champ, and me," Lucy said, smiling.

"You, Champ, and Me," the song that was in her dream, had a lineage back to Lucy's long, lost mother. Papa sang the chorus with Lucy's mother when she was a little girl. Lucy and Papa wrote some new verses to the song.

Papa grabbed his beat-up guitar again. Everything Papa had, seemed old and beat-up: his boat, his guitar, his books, his cabin.

24

He told Lucy that he was like the ancient Israelites who wore the same shoes walking through the desert for forty years.

Papa hit the first chord, strumming a G chord again and singing their song,

> *I saw in your bright eyes*
> *The light of the fireflies*
> *We can stay in Bulwagga Bay*
> *On our ship we'll sail away...*

Lucy loved her Papa very much. Sometimes she worried about him since he was sixty years-old. Her school teacher, Miss Marino, said the average lifespan of a man is approximately seventy years-old, which troubled Lucy, because she didn't want to lose Papa in ten years like she lost her parents. When she sang the Champ song that her Mama used to sing "You, Champ, and Me," the music always helped her feel better.

Lucy broke into singing the chorus with Papa, snapping her fingers as she sang,

> *Lake Lady,*
> *We'll live on our boat upon the sea,*
> *Just you, Champ, and me...*

Papa put the guitar down so his hands were free. Lucy and Papa danced together. Lucy stood on his toes as their voices rang out in the humble cabin, and sang:

> *Since you called my name*
> *I haven't been the same*
> *I spend all night on Lake Champlain*

"Pick me up, Papa" Lucy said. He lifted Lucy up in his arms and they danced as they sang:

Lucy & the Lake Monster

We're entwined by design
Searching until we find
The legend of the lake that transcends time...

Papa said a silent prayer, asking for the secrets of the sea serpent, the legend that transcends time, to be revealed to Lucy.

Chapter 4
A Trip to Town

On an average Saturday morning, Papa Jerry and little Lucy set out to find Champ. As the sun rose in the sky above the Lake Champlain cedar pines, Lucy's hopes raised, too. The winter snow melted, forming raging mountain streams that raised the water levels of the lake.

Lucy brought along her green dinosaur toy from Champ's Trading Post for good luck. She just knew in her heart that Champ was real, and she trusted her heart more than anything anybody else could say.

Papa and Lucy walked through Port Henry, the town near Bulwagga Bay where many people claimed to have seen Champ. Lucy smelled the strange, wild smell of the wet leaves and bark from the rain-laden trees. Gray squirrels scurried around them, retrieving the nuts they'd hidden in holes close to their tree nests.

The sulfur egglike smell from the A & J Paper Plant, in a neighboring town south of Port Henry, drifted by in the south wind. Papa inhaled the redolence of the mill and remembered working there for decades on Packaging Line Seven in the Finishing Room. A half-dozen rolls of paper came down the conveyors and the cutters cut them into copy paper. Papa performed the machine-like, mind-numbing task of slicing them and stacking them in a box. Papa noticed some paper split and went to the left and some to the right where they were labelled differently before they were shipped to Warehouse 54. The pricey brand cost more than the paper labelled with a generic moniker, yet it was the same paper.

Lucy & the Lake Monster

Profit took precedence over honesty and ethics, Papa thought to himself, remembering. He sensed he and Lucy were about to encounter that same mercenary mindset opposing them in their search for Champ.

He thought about that often, how people, like the paper at the mill, are valued based on a label. Reporters and skeptics labeled Lucy and Papa as less intelligent than them, an old eccentric and his granddaughter, yet Papa knew they were just as valuable as the "normies," as Lucy called them.

Papa snapped out of his recollection as they walked into the Town Square on Main Street. He pointed to a big, green statue of the sea serpent Champ.

"Look, Lucy."

Lucy's eyes popped out. "Wow! It's really pretty."

"I think it's pretty, too," Papa said, although 'pretty' wouldn't be the word he would've chosen to describe Champ.

"Isn't it humongous, Papa?"

"Yes, it is humongous," Papa said, smiling and chuckling.

Lucy's mouth opened wide. "I wonder how they got a picture of Champ to model for that and how did they make him stay still so long?"

Papa laughed at this, imagining Champ posing still for a picture. "You think of questions no one else thinks of, Lucy."

Lucy's whole body squirmed with excitement. Her legs started moving out from under her and she ran to the Champ statue and gave him a big hug.

"Do you think that's what Champ looks like, big and green with a smile on his face?" Papa asked.

Lucy stepped back to get a better look at Champ. "Well...how do I know if this is what Champ looks like?"

"I remember you told me you had a dream about Champ, Lucy. Does the statue look similar to your dream?" Papa asked.

Lucy looked up, remembering her dreams. "Pretty much, with some differences."

"Like what, Lucy?"

"In my dreams of Champ, he was majestical and green. Green like a green garbage bag," Lucy said, giggling. "This statue is cool, but it's just painted one lighter shade of green. In my dreams, he's a mixture of greens, like spinach and algae mixed together, but overall, a darker green." Lucy flicked her hair back with her hand.

Papa marveled at Lucy's ability to notice details. "What about Champ's body?"

"He was snake-shaped like that, but he had more scales, and he was way bigger in my dreams."

"Ah-ha," Papa said. "That's a good point. The cryptozoologists are people who study animals whose existence hasn't been proven. They agree Champ is really big, like an underwater dinosaur that can swim. So, this statue looks like him in some ways, but not in other ways?"

"Different statues look a little different. I don't know which one is the right one that looks the most like him. This body is wood, so it's stiff, because it's a statue. In my dreams, he has green flesh," Lucy said. She smiled and paused for a few seconds.

Lucy & the Lake Monster

"What about the head?" Papa said, smiling.

"He had two more sets of horns on his head."

"Oh, two more, huh?" Papa put his hand to his chin and thought. "What did the horns look like?

"Your average Viking horns. Curved cow horns," Lucy said, curving her hands and fingers above her head to demonstrate. "They were big in the front, then smaller in the back of Champ's head."

"What else do you like about this statue?"

"Well...I like that it makes him nice, with a smile. His smile is absolutely the way I dreamt it would be."

"Do you think his teeth are like that?"

"His teeth look a little sharp on this statue. I don't think his teeth are sharp like a carnivore that eats meat. Maybe he's just a plant eater under the water. He has flat teeth, like an herbivore."

"Why do you think he's a plant eater?"

"If he was a predator, there would be a decline of certain marine animals in the food chain. I learned that in science."

"Your teacher, Miss Marino, would be proud of you."

"I like the scales on his back, too," Lucy said.

She looked away from the statue to the other side of the street. She heard a striped skunk scurrying towards a shade tree. The skunk's potent odor assaulted Lucy's nostrils, overcoming the rotten egg smell of the paper mill.

Richard Rossi & Kelly Tabor

Across the street was a mean-looking, eight-foot-tall statue of Champ, the opposite of the friendly statue near Papa and Lucy. It was made by a man Papa called "Mercenary Mike" and his girlfriend Beezel Beemish, also known as B.B. Lucy looked over to their demonic Champ statue.

Mercenary Mike Mueller was a greasy-haired loud-mouth. He and his bleached blonde girlfriend Beezel Beemish were a couple in Bulwagga Bay who were hunting for Champ, like Lucy and Papa, but they were out for money. That's why Papa had nicknamed him "Mercenary" Mike.

When Lucy had once asked Papa what "mercenary" meant, Papa said to "Look it up in the dictionary, Lucy. Remember leaders are readers."

When Lucy looked up "mercenary," she found this definition in the dictionary:

"Concerned only with making money at the expense of ethics of what is right or wrong."

Mercenary Mike and Beezel spread rumors that Champ was a vicious monster they had to capture to keep the townspeople safe. They had stalked Lucy's mother, following her as she looked for Champ, and now Mike and Beezel did the same to Papa and Lucy.

Lucy felt a creepy feeling around Beezel and Mercenary Mike, like they were two satanic snakes after her and Papa, just like the old devil was after Adam and Eve. *They know more than they let on,* Lucy thought. There was something mysterious about them, a mystery Lucy wanted to solve one day. She looked away from Mercenary Mike's mean Champ statue and looked closer at the friendly Champ statue again.

Lucy & the Lake Monster

"In my dreams, Champ doesn't have wheels like this statue has, Papa."

"There's going to be a big Champ Day at the Bulwagga Bay campground. Your Mama started the first Champ Day years ago," Papa said. "It's kept going ever since. The City Council made that statue for a float in the parade. The wheels help it move down the street."

"Can we go to the parade, Papa?"

"That'll be fun, Lucy. At the parade, people dress up like Champ. Merchants sell Champ trinkets and toys. There'll probably be games and Champ stuff and yummy food." Papa smiled and his eyes lit up like a child.

"Can I get a hot dog with ketchup?" Lucy said. "Or better yet, one of Annie's Michigan Dogs with meat sauce?"

"Yes!" Papa said. "On Champ Day they call them 'Champ Dogs.'" Lucy laughed, her eyes twinkling and her heart filled with fun at the thought of "Champ Dogs."

Mercenary Mike and Beezel were jealous of Champ Day and the attention it got in the local newspaper, so they started their own Champ Day across the street in Mike and Beezel's driveway. They called it by the different name of "Champalooza."

As Papa and Lucy walked through town, they heard Beezel Beemish yelling at people passing by through a bullhorn in her scratchy voice. Her screechy voice grew closer as Beezel and Mercenary Mike walked down her driveway to the end, near the dock, just twenty feet from Papa and Lucy.

Beezel was big and bulky, with a bulbous nose that was red at the tip. She had stringy bleached hair, wild like a witch's hair, craggy as a crow's nest. She wore too much makeup, which looked like red circle blotches on her cheeks and her eyes, making her face look like a creepy clown.

Mercenary Mike, her boyfriend, looked like he needed a good bath. He had red welts in a zigzag pattern on his skin from sleeping with bed bugs. Lucy smelled a second putrid aroma, in addition to the foul smell of the skunk. Mercenary had horrid body odor, the rancid smell of stale fish from the lake, mingled with the stench of bad breath and Beezel Beemish on him. He stunk so bad Lucy gagged when she whiffed his putrid odor, combined with the skunk's stink still filling the air. Mercenary's dark hair was unwashed, and his head infested with flakes of dandruff and head lice. He had big, black bags under his eyes.

He needs to brush his teeth, wash his hair, and put on some clean clothes, Lucy thought. Her thoughts were interrupted by a booming voice splitting the air.

"Don't come to the second-rate sideshow of Champ Day," Beezel bellowed from the corner of the dock. Mercenary Mike was standing beside her. "Come to *our* Champalooza instead. We will give you FREE Champ hot dogs and hamburgers and not charge you for food the way Champ Day does. Don't go to the other Champ Day because it's the enemy's camp."

"You tell 'em, Beemish," Mercenary Mike said. He had a strange habit of calling everyone by their last name, even his own girlfriend. It was one of the ways he tried to act tough. He never got close enough to anyone to use their first name. Beezel had a strange habit of calling everyone "Toots."

Beezel accused Champ Day of being out for money, when her and Mike were the ones making money off Champ. Papa called this "projection." Champ Day gave any proceeds they made back to poor children. Champalooza gave proceeds into the pockets of Mercenary Mike and B.B.

Lucy & the Lake Monster

Lucy looked over at Beezel for a moment, and saw she was surrounded by posters and banners about "Champalooza." The banners read:

CHAMPALOOZA
HOSTED BY THE REAL LAKE LADY: BEEZEL BEEMISH
The World's Greatest Champ Expert who has Appeared
On TV, Radio, Internet, and Film Documentaries
With Co-Host and Champ Hunter Michael Mueller

Their eight-foot-tall, scary statue of Champ hovered beside Beezel Beemish and Mercenary Mike. Their fake Champ had a mean, monster face, with bigger, sharper teeth. It matched the ugly monster faces of Mercenary Mike and Beezel. Lucy didn't like it.

"*Whenever Champ has made himself known*," Lucy thought, "*he's never hurt anybody.*"

"Come to my Champ Store and get my books about Champ, and my Champ documentaries," Beezel said. "Meet my partner Mike and me, the world's foremost Champ experts in person."

"For a small fee, we will autograph our Champ books and documentaries," Mercenary Mike said.

He was lying about the fee being small. They charged high prices so they could outfit their expensive Champ houseboat.

"We have new Champ coffee cups that change colors to the green of Champ's skin when you pour in your drink," Beezel said. "Come and buy my Champ soaps and candles."

"We got Champ everything," Mercenary Mike said, directing his voice at Lucy. "For just fifty dollars, I'll give you a tour of our Champ boat. See the equipment I'm gonna use to capture that monster Champ."

"No!" Lucy cried, panicked at the thought of anyone capturing her beloved Champ.

"Hey, little Lucy Lago! You want to buy some Champ stuff?" Mercenary Mike said.

"No," Lucy said again firmly.

"You and your rickety grandpa want to tour a real boat, Toots?" Beezel said in a cranky voice.

"No! Nope! Never!" Lucy said.

"I thought you like Champ, Lago?" Mercenary Mike said.

"I don't just like Champ, I LOVE Champ," Lucy said with spunk and spirit. "He is NOT a monster for you to capture, so, stop looking for him."

"He's gentle," Papa said. "He's more afraid of us than we are of him."

"I'm not afraid of Champ, old man. I'm excited to be singing all the way to the bank when I deposit all the money I make for capturing that beast," Mercenary Mike sneered.

"When WE deposit all the money, Toots," Beezel said.

Papa reached into his pocket and pulled out the formal decree the local legislature passed. He read aloud:

"In 1981, the legislature of Port Henry formally decreed the waters of Lake Champlain are a safe haven for Champ. In 1982, the bordering state of Vermont passed a House Resolution protecting Champ from capture, kidnap, or harm. In 1983, the state of New York's state Assembly and the state Senate passed resolutions to protect Champ from mercenary attempts to

Lucy & the Lake Monster

capture him." Papa folded the paper and put it back in his pocket.

"You're NEVER going to capture Champ!" Lucy said.

"That's what you think, Toots," Beezel said, "and you don't scare me Lago with your little laws protecting your Champy. I got fancy lawyers looking for loopholes and I'm gonna make so much money off that beast I can fight in court until the cows come home!"

Some bystanders looked over, shaking their heads at how B.B. and Mercenary Mike were harassing Lucy, so Beezel continued her sales pitch through her bullhorn.

"Come and see our biggest, best boat with the biggest, best equipment to find Champ. Buy your tickets to board our boat." Her voice got louder and louder. "COME JOIN THE FUN!" Beezel screamed.

It made Lucy and Papa feel sick to their stomach to see how Beezel and Mercenary Mike were using fear of Champ to make money. They walked faster and faster to get away from the sound of Beezel's screechy screams. Beezel Beemish made Lucy squeamish.

Beezel's jealousy of Lucy's mother Lynn Lago and her Champ Day went back a long time ago to their school days when they were classmates. She hated Lucy's mother because she was the prettiest and most popular girl at Crown Point High School, home of the mighty Panthers. Beezel was so spoiled and self-centered, she didn't like any other girls getting praise that took attention from her.

Mercenary Mike tried to date Lynn, but she was not interested. She knew, even then, his heart was darker than his dark, greasy hair. Beezel liked Mike, even back in high school, and she hated that he was more attracted to Lynn than to her.

The green-eyed monster had Beezel by the throat. She was jealous of Lynn's long, naturally wavy blonde hair, so she bleached her own dark hair blonde to look like her. Lynn beat her out for head cheerleader, captain of the Panthers soccer and softball teams, and student body president. Lynn wasn't trying to outdo Beezel, she was just blessed with more talent and natural beauty.

Lynn and Beezel both looked for Champ, but Lynn was the one who was in the newspapers for her search.

Beezel and Mercenary Mike made false claims several years ago to get headlines for themselves, but it backfired. They claimed to have photos and videos of Champ, as well as audio evidence for Champ's underwater sounds captured through sonar.

Their claims were investigated, and they were busted for faking the Champ pictures. They created the fakes on Photoshop. Their video footage of Champ was debunked as CGI, (computer-generated imagery). They were exposed for faking Champ sounds with an audio computer app and a keyboard synthesizer that made animal noises with different sound chips.

Since Lynn's boating accident, Beezel Beemish bragged that she was taking Lynn's place as the Champ expert.

"Now, I am the number one Champ researcher in the whole world. I'm carrying on my best friend Lynn Lago's work. As soon as she died, I sent flowers, of course," Beezel said with a grin, trying to make herself appear better than she really was.

Beezel's insincerity bugged Papa and Lucy because they knew how much Beezel always despised Lucy's mother, due to her own insecurities. After Lynn died, Beezel lied and said they were good friends, even though she was her nemesis. She never sent any flowers.

Papa and Lucy walked further down Main Street, shaking the dust off their feet. B.B.'s voice faded softer and softer as they distanced themselves. They felt the sunlight on their face, and their faith strengthened, with each step away from the devilish duo.

Chapter 5
Signs and Wonders

Papa and Lucy continued walking and came to the intersection with Whitney Street.

"Oh, there's the Bulwagga Bay sign I told you about," Papa said, excited as he pointed to the historical marker. "Those people are all eyewitnesses. The sign has their names and the dates they saw Champ."

The sign stood proudly along New York 9N and Whitney. At the center board of the sign was a drawing of Champ that showed his green, snakelike body and tail coming out of the water of Lake Champlain. The drawing was underneath the words:

CHAMP SIGHTINGS
IN BULWAGGA BAY AREA

Below and on both sides of the Champ drawing were names and dates of sightings, starting with Samuel de Champlain in 1609.

Lucy sighed and smiled. "I love looking at this sign," Lucy said. "So many people have seen Champ, more than I ever imagined."

"It is a lot of names, Lucy. More than three hundred people saw Champ. Over the span of four centuries."

"That's a lot, Papa."

"As the number of settlers in this area grew, the number of sightings of Champ grew."

Lucy & the Lake Monster

"My name's gonna be up there someday, Papa." She pointed to the top row and said, "Way up there."

Papa smiled. Lucy looked at all the names of hundreds of people who said they saw Champ, scanning from top to bottom. Lucy read a few names out loud:

Bess Sherlock 5-69
Lynn Williams 4-19-81
Ronald Baker 4-19-81
Sue Cutting 4-29-81
Paul Cutting 4-29-81
Louis Trapasso 8-74
Camilla Rich 4-17-81

"Why isn't Mama's name on there?" Lucy asked.

"Your mother was trying to get pictures of Champ. I don't know if her camera is still around somewhere, but if it is, I want to see the film that's in it," Papa said. Deep down, he had hoped her camera survived the boat wreck, but when the police returned her personal effects, there was no camera.

"Do you think it could have pictures of Champ?" Lucy asked, wide-eyed.

"Your mother was an excellent photographer, and she was more driven than anyone I know to find Champ. So, there's a good chance."

"If you and Mama saw Champ, your names should be on the sign," Lucy insisted.

"She and I both had sightings, but we wanted to have solid proof because there are a lot of doubters. Champ comes up for just a moment, and you see his long neck and humps, briefly. Then he disappears back into the depths, just as quick as he came, leaving you looking at the lake, hoping for another glimpse." Papa demonstrated this with his hands going up and down. "An old guy like me, I'm not too quick with a cellphone to get pictures. You'll be much better at it than I am, Lucy."

"Do all these people on the sign have solid proof and photos?"

"No, they don't, Lucy. Their sightings are no better than your mother's or mine. All these names believe Champ is real."

"Do you believe they're all real, Papa?"

"I don't know all the people and their stories personally. I can't say with one hundred percent certainty they're all real. There are names of people I know personally, so I can vouch for some of them. They feel confident they saw Champ. They don't seem to be making it up, but it's their word against the cynics. They're telling their story, which is called *anecdotal evidence*."

"What's *anecdotal*, Papa?"

"An anecdote is a story. Your mother and I decided we wanted evidence to back up our story to the skeptics before we allowed our names to be on the sign. Anecdotal evidence is not enough, that's why your mother was looking for more proof." Papa got choked up for a moment. "When the accident happened, her research and film disappeared. You're like your mother, Lucy, and we can take over where she left off."

Lucy patted Papa's back to comfort him. "Your name should be on there too, Papa," Lucy said, repeating herself as she was prone to do.

"Thank you," Papa said. His eyes lit up at the thought. "I hope your name gets on that sign someday, Lucy."

Lucy & the Lake Monster

"I hope so too, Papa."

"I did see him once, but like I said, I didn't want to put my name on the sign until I had better proof. Maybe it's easier now with cellphone cameras. We didn't have those back in my day."

"You and I will get better proof and a picture, Papa. I promise you."

Papa smiled the biggest smile of the day. "Thank you, Sweetie."

Lucy scanned the names and dates on the sign again. "The years on the sign for when people saw Champ are sooooo long ago."

"Yes, that's true, Lucy. Plus, the sign is already full with names with no more room."

"They're gonna have to make more signs to make room for our names and other people who see Champ in the future," Lucy said, bursting into a humongous grin from ear to ear.

"Yes, definitely," Papa said. "They need to get some wood panels and make that sign bigger to put our names on it when we see Champ. More sightings deserve more signs."

"Papa, I want our names to be in gold, because I'm determined," Lucy said, as she bounced up and down like a ball. Lucy pretended she was writing on the sign with her finger, pantomiming large, loopy letters. "Lucy and Papa," she said as she played air-writing. "I've been looking for Champ my whole life. I'll find him. I've dreamed of seeing him. We'll show all the normies that make fun of us. One of these days." Lucy's face filled with fullness of joy at the thought as she looked up.

"One of these days," Papa said.

"Some of the names have the same dates, Papa."

"Yes, that's because family members saw Champ on the same day, usually in the warmer months, during lake outings."

"Tell me again what you saw, Papa?"

Papa repeated his story many times to Lucy, but he didn't mind telling her again. "When I was fishing for pike, Lucy, I saw movement in the water."

"What was it?"

"A wake, followed by two black humps. I believe it was Champ, but some friends and people in town mocked me and said, 'It was just a lake sturgeon.' You see, Lucy, sturgeons are very large fish, as long as our boat, ol' skiff, up to twelve feet long and fifty-five pounds."

"That's bigger than me, Papa."

"Sturgeon sometimes are mistaken for Champ, but your Mama believed in Champ and so do I."

"Oh my goodness, that will be so cool when we see Champ again. Our family will get up there on the sign, for all to see." Lucy smiled, with a heavenly glow just thinking about it.

"One member of our family's already there. Your Uncle Bob is on the sign, Robert Blye. Actually, he's your great-uncle. He owns Captain Blye's Restaurant a couple blocks from here on Bulwagga Bay. Many people in his restaurant claim to have seen Champ, so he keeps binoculars on the tables so customers can hopefully catch a glimpse of our little Champy."

Lucy found Uncle Bob's name on the first panel of the three-paneled sign and read it aloud.

Lucy & the Lake Monster

Robert Blye 7-8-75

"Maybe this will be the day we see Champ," Lucy said, as she looked to the lake in the distance.

"Maybe," Papa answered. "Speaking of Uncle Bob, would you like to stop at Captain Blye's and get some lunch?"

"That sounds great, Papa. Do people believe Uncle Bob's story?"

"Some people doubt it."

"Why?"

"Maybe I shouldn't say it, because you're a little girl, but some of the guys at Uncle Bob's restaurant sit at the bar and tip back a few. Some people say Uncle Bob had one too many and that's the reason he saw Champ." Papa laughed. "I shouldn't say that. Your Uncle Bob's a great man with a wonderful restaurant. Aunt Joan's known for her tasty vittles. Now, when we go in there to eat, just stay close to me, Sunshine."

"Okay, Papa."

Chapter 6
Captain Blye's

When they walked into Captain Blye's restaurant to eat lunch, Papa looked around, more cautiously than usual. He held Lucy's hand extra tight.

The restaurant was in a boat house. The tables were by big windows overlooking Bulwagga Bay. Customers peered through binoculars at the bay, looking for a glimpse of the elusive Champ. A green sculpture of Champ was in a small pond, just behind the restaurant. The furnishings were maroon and mahogany, imparting an elegance to the rough-and-tumble crowd.

Captain Blye, Lucy's great uncle, had been a drummer on the ocean liners to Europe in his younger days. He played Ludwig drums with brushes while his sister, Betty, played jazz piano in the corner of the restaurant. She was tickling the ivories, playing a twelve-bar boogie-woogie blues.

"Stay close to me, Lucy," Papa said again, repeating his earlier warning. "There's some tipsy characters in this place." Papa's eyes zeroed in on Mister Brook.

Mister Brook was an older man with a funny smell. He wore a crooked sailor hat and his shirt was stained with spilled drinks. He sat at the counter all day refilling his glass until he slurred his words. The more Mister Brook drank, the more he talked about seeing Champ, but the people of Port Henry dismissed his stories.

The villagers knew about Papa and Lucy's belief in Champ. When her mother died, looking for him, reporters showed up at their cabin to interview them. Lucy and Papa had said if Mama died looking for Champ, he must be real.

Mister Brook attempted to get Lucy's attention. "Hey, Lucy!" He winked to Lucy and said, "Three of these, and I guarantee you'll see Champ."

"No thank you," Papa said, waving his hand dismissively.

"No sir," Lucy said, shaking her head back and forth, from side to side.

The wobbly man raised his glass to Lucy to take a sip. "Hey, dontchu just want to have one, Lucy?" he said, slurring his words. Papa felt his blood begin to boil because he wanted to protect Lucy. "You'll see Champ, guaranteed. Take a sip, take a sip!"

Papa didn't look at the man. He held her hand tighter and led her away from him quickly, removing her from the situation.

"No thank you, Mister Brook," Lucy said, looking over her shoulder as they walked away. "I don't want to get sick. Besides, I'm more in the mood for a root beer."

"Good for you, Lucy," Papa said. "Just keep walking and let's get us a seat." Papa didn't want Lucy lingering in the tavern section.

"Hold on just a second, okay," Mister Brook said, pointing and staggering closer towards them. Brook kept rambling as Papa took Lucy away from him and shot him a look. "I'm not inebriated, all right? I can even spell it, but don't ask me to spell it now. A, B, B, R, E..." Mister Brook said, realizing he couldn't spell. "I want to tell you, I saw the sea serpent, and you can see it too, with just a little drinkie-poo. Don't you and your grandpa want to see Champ?"

Then, she looked up to Papa and whispered out of the left side of her mouth. "Papa? What's with that guy?"

"That's an example of why I gave up drinking a long time ago," Papa said.

Brook kept talking to himself. "The police occifer drives me home sometimes," Mister Brook said, slurring his words and mispronouncing 'officer' as 'occifer.' "The more I drink, the more I see Champ all day long. I see him all the time, my friend, all the time."

Papa and Lucy scurried away by a few booths where people ate their food and watched them. "What was *that*, Papa?"

"It's a running joke in Port Henry that some of the men in Captain Blye's see Champ the more they drink. People don't believe Mister Brook's stories because his visions are more in his glass than in the lake."

Lucy leaned close to Papa and whispered. "Just between you and me, I think he's crazy, Papa."

"I'd agree with you there, Lucy," Papa said. "When he's not drinking, he can be a pleasant person. What he's drinking is making him seem crazy. I'm sorry about that, Lucy."

"That's okay, Papa."

"He's someone we can pray for," Papa said. "I'm not proud of it, but I was like him years ago. I was powerless to stop drinking. You know what, Lucy?"

"Yes, Papa?"

Lucy & the Lake Monster

"Someone prayed for me, and that someone was your mother, when she was a little girl like you. I haven't had a drop since."

"Still looking for Champ?" Sam the Scientist called to them from a nearby white linen table in the fancy dining area. Sam was feeling superior because he recently won an award for his research papers in zoology. He wore geeky, dark-framed glasses and a white lab coat with a pen and laser pointer in his pocket. He carried hand sanitizer and wore plastic gloves because he was germ-phobic. "Didn't you know plesiosaurs are extinct?"

"Who says Champ is a plesio-" Lucy said, struggling to pronounce the big word. "Plesyabob, or whatever you said." *One day I'll be able to pronounce that word*, Lucy thought to herself.

"I can understand a child's faith, but you're a grown man, Lago," Sam said to Papa.

"Unless you become like a little child, you cannot see," Papa said.

Two reporters, tall and lanky Roger Melnick, and short and stout Karl Kane scribbled in their notebooks as they sipped drinks at a nearby table.

"Any luck finding the monster, Lago?" Melnick said, smirking.

"He's not a monster," Lucy said.

"We're going out on the lake later," Papa said.

Kane and Melnick snickered in mockery as Papa and Lucy found their seat. Lucy knew that the "normal" people, who she derisively called the "normies," ridiculed her and Papa for their beat-up rowboat, their ramshackle cabin, and their quest to find Champ.

"Good luck, Lago the lake loon," Kane said. "If you get proof of Champ, I challenge you to come down to the newspaper office and subject it to scrutiny. If you pass muster, we'll put you on the front page."

"The day the Lagos are on the front page is the day pigs fly," Melnick added, chuckling.

"You don't have a prayer, Lago," Sam the Scientist said.

"Come down to the shore. See for yourself when Papa and I go out later in our boat," Lucy said.

"We'll be there," Melnick said.

Deep down, as much as she didn't like the "normies," Lucy felt she needed their approval. She needed to show them her and Papa were right, and that the normies were no better than them.

She shook this feeling off and thought to herself, *Who wants to be a normie anyways?*

A third reporter, the one honest and fair writer in town, Larry Lore, waved hi to Papa and Lucy and smiled.

Lucy waved back. "Have a Champtastic day," Lucy said.

They sat down at a booth with red-checkered tablecloths and looked through the binoculars out at Bulwagga Bay. The Bay was the place where there were more sightings of Champ than anywhere else. Lake Champlain was sparkling, inviting them to explore.

"The water looks blue," Lucy said.

Lucy & the Lake Monster

"Blue is the color of my eyes, and the eyes of my Lucy," Papa said. "The color of the sky, and the color of the sea."

"Blue is the color of the eyes of Papa and me," Lucy answered. "The color of the sky, and the color of the sea."

"Do you see anything yet, Lucy?" Papa asked, as they peered through binoculars to the bay. He looked out at Sandy Beach and saw kids on kayaks and canoes.

"No, but I see a fisherman pulling in a big fish," Lucy said, looking through the lens of her binoculars.

"Oh yeah, that's Mike Leicher. Looks like he got himself a nice Northern Pike," Papa said.

Papa scanned the lake with his binoculars. He watched some fishermen seek round or rainbow fish, while others sought carp or catfish. He knew that many of his fisherman friends made fun of him and his ol' skiff, but he never held it against them.

"I just saw a fish jumping out of the water," Lucy said. "It was so cute!"

"They jump up to get bugs to eat," Papa said. "Oh sorry, I don't want to ruin your appetite." Lucy laughed. "Speaking of appetite, what would you like for lunch, Lucy? Eating will give us more strength to look for Champ."

"So... if I eat, do you think I have a better chance of seeing Champ?"

"Yes, you sure do have a better chance. I'm sorry we didn't get out on the lake earlier like we had planned. You know how I am. I threw out my watch and I run late sometimes. Let's order to get our strength up to look for Champ this afternoon. What would you like to eat, Lucy?"

"Hmmmm. Let me see," Lucy said, putting down the binoculars and thinking about how good Aunt Joan cooked her favorite meals. "I'm craving mac and cheese."

"Yummy. Aunt Joan makes it really good, Lucy."

"Is she in back? In the kitchen?"

"Yes."

"Aunt Joan's the best cook. She makes the best mac and cheese and tomato soup."

"It's an old family recipe," Papa said, smiling.

"What are you gonna have, Papa?"

"Steak and cheese sandwich. I like how Aunt Joan slices the steak really thin and melts the cheese."

"I don't really like that," Lucy said.

"You better stick with mac and cheese then," Papa said, smiling. Papa loved Lucy so much he adored how she talked about ordinary things like Mac and cheese.

"Hey, both our lunches end with 'and cheese,' Papa. You got steak and cheese. I got mac and cheese."

"We may be different, but deep down we're the same, Lucy," Papa said

Lucy looked up and saw the waitress with a pad and pencil in her hands. She was chunky and had a brassy, clarion voice. She kept her pencil behind her ear until it was time to write the food order.

Lucy & the Lake Monster

"Hey you two," the waitress said. "What would you like to order, Hon? Joan can cook up anything you want in the kitchen."

"I'd like some mac and cheese, tomato soup, and some Lake Monster fries," Lucy said.

"Would you like those fries loaded with everything on them?" the waitress said, in her twangy voice.

"What does that mean?" Lucy asked.

"I add cheese and bacon," she said.

"Yes, please. Sounds great," Lucy said. "And Papa will take a steak and cheese sandwich."

"Okay." She scribbled on her small notepad. "Would you like oyster crackers with your tomato soup, Lucy?"

"Yes, please."

"Okay. I'll bring you extra," the waitress said with a warm smile. "What would you like to drink with that?"

"Ice water for me," Papa said.

"I'll take a root beer!" Lucy said. "Thank you."

"You're welcome," the waitress said. "Is that all you would like, Pretty Lady?"

"Yes," Lucy said, giggling at the compliment. "Papa, she called me Pretty Lady."

"That's because you're the prettiest little girl anyone's ever seen on God's green earth," Papa said.

"Yes, she's absolutely beautiful," the waitress said. "You're the prettiest girl who's ever come into Captain Blye's. It's so good to see you again, Jerry. And to see your granddaughter. I remember her Mama coming into the restaurant. And Lucy looks very much like her beautiful mother."

"Thank you for remembering her," Papa said, his voice quivering.

She saw Papa and Lucy were touched by this, almost as if they could cry, so she changed the subject.

"I'm so sorry to eavesdrop, but I overheard you say earlier that you are going out to find Champ," the waitress said. "Your Aunt Joan and I want you to have enough food on that boat, so we're gonna pack up some sandwiches for you here. I promise I won't pack any tuna because I don't want to scare any fish away in case you're fishing." She grinned.

"I already packed some Fluffernutters in my backpack," Lucy said.

"Fluffernutters?" the waitress said.

"My favorite sandwich in the whole world," Lucy said. "Peanut butter and marshmallow creme."

"Sounds delicious. Knowing you two, you might be hunting Champ into late evening, so I'll pack some additional food to go with your Fluffernutters," the waitress said. "Oh, I just got some fresh apples I'll pack, too. An apple a day, keeps the doctor away."

"And it makes our Champy come our way," Lucy said, showing off her quick wit.

Lucy & the Lake Monster

"Amen. Thanks," Papa said. "We're much obliged. We're gonna be out there several hours and we're gonna work up an appetite."

"I'll be back with your food in a jiffy," she said as she scurried back to the kitchen.

A bus boy brought a basket of biscuits and butter, along with Lucy's root beer and Papa's water. Shortly after, the waitress brought their lunch to the table. Papa and Lucy joined hands and Papa bowed his head and prayed aloud.

"We thank Thee, O Lord, who bringeth forth food from the sea for us all. For what we're about to receive, we are truly grateful, for it is from Thy bounty, through Christ our Lord, Amen."

Papa was about to make the sign of the cross, when Lucy whispered with her childlike faith, "P.S. God, just one more thing. Thank You for loving Mister Brook. Help him stop drinking. He needs Your mercy and grace, Amen."

"Amen," Papa said, "you have a beautiful heart, that's a beautiful prayer. It reminds me of something your mother might have prayed."

Lucy smiled. "Let's dig in," she said, as they started eating.

Chapter 7
Lago Time

During lunch, Lucy and Papa sat at their table at Captain Blye's and talked. Papa had an idea that made him smile.

"Lucy, I want to treat you to a gift. Since we don't make it into town very often, let's make it a special day. You're getting a new dress! What color would you like?"

"Blue! My favorite color," Lucy said.

"The ocean is blue and the sky is blue," Papa said.

"Blue is the color of the eyes of Papa and me," Lucy said, smiling. "The color of the sky, and the color of the sea."

"The color of my eyes, and the eyes of my Lucy," Papa said, returning her smile and repeating their verbal ritual.

"I like dresses, and I need one for when they have a dance at school, but I don't want to wear them all the time. I like dungarees and overalls like you wear, and Bella chewed up my jeans."

"Bella chewed your jeans?" Papa laughed. "Then I'll buy you those, too. What kind do you want?"

Lucy smiled. "The kind with patches on the knees."

"What else would you like, Bright Eyes?"

"I don't want you to spend too much. Besides, money doesn't grow on trees."

"I want to. Whatever you want, Papa will get it for you. Tell me something else you'd like to wear?"

"Can I get a Champ tee-shirt?"

"You sure can, sweetie. That's a great idea. They have Champ tee-shirts with a cartoon Champ on the front. They also have Champ hats to keep your face protected from the sun when we go out on the lake." Papa smiled, seeing the excitement in Lucy's eyes.

"Woohoo," Lucy said. "What color are the Champ hats and shirts?"

"Green."

"Awesome! The color of Champ's skin," Lucy said. "Like a green garbage bag. When he sees my Champ shirt and hat, he'll know I'm his friend and I'm not gonna hurt him." Lucy played with her green Champ toy, moving it on the red-checkered table.

"Do you know what size tee-shirt you wear, Lucy?"

"I think I might be a medium."

"Medium. Okay. It seems like just yesterday you were a little baby. We can get sunscreen to protect us from sunburn, too," Papa said.

"Is the sunscreen fifty or one hundred?" Lucy asked.

"I don't know. What's better, Sunshine?" Papa said.

"One hundred UVA protection," Lucy said, laughing a little at Papa's question and how sometimes she knew more about some things than he did.

"Okay, I'll get one hundred protection." Papa paused, thinking about the different stores on Main Street. "Next door to the Five & Dime Store is a nail salon. Would you like a manicure?"

"What exactly do they do at a nail salon?" Lucy asked, laughing.

"That's where women go to get their fingernails done up real pretty."

"Ahhh, no. We can just do that at home, Papa. Besides, this boy in my class says he loves me, Ricky Taschner. He also loves to play baseball and he's teaching me during recess how to pitch. If I make my nails too long, I won't be able to throw very good."

"Okay, no pretty nails. Let's not disappoint Ricky Taschner and hurt your softball career. Would you like to get the Champ Monster Banana Split at Stewart's?" Papa said, using his hands to make circles like scoops of ice cream. "It has strawberry, chocolate, vanilla, mint chocolate chip, plus whipped cream, bananas, and nuts, too. On the top are little horns and eyeballs to look like Champ's face. And last but not least, a cherry on top."

"Yes! They say it's so big no one's been able to finish it, Papa. It looks like a real monster with horns and eyeballs."

"It's HUGE. We can get two spoons. You can start eating from one end, and I'll start at the other until we meet in the middle," Papa said, making motions like he was spooning ice cream into his mouth.

"That's the BEST idea, Papa! That sounds AMAZING!" Lucy squealed with anticipation. "It's so humongous, I don't know if we can, but we can try Papa. I ate a whole container of mint chocolate ice cream once, so I think I can handle it." Lucy had a determined look in her eyes. She remembered mint chocolate was not just her favorite flavor, but her mother's favorite flavor, too.

"You think you can handle it, Lucy?"

"I bet I can finish it," Lucy said, grinning. Papa laughed. Lucy's joy was contagious.

Papa had worked twelve hour shifts at the A & J Paper Plant for forty years, then retired. He didn't think of the mill much anymore, unless the south wind was blowing just right, and the rotten-eggs smell from the chemicals wafted by. The paper mill gave him a retirement watch and a card that said, "CONGRATULATIONS, JERRY LAGO." Later that night when he was alone, Papa threw out the watch and said he wasn't "bound by time anymore."

"No appointments, no schedules. No have-tos, supposed-tos, and shoulds," Papa had said. "I'm living on Lago Time now."

"Lago Time" became a phrase between Lucy and Papa to mean they didn't have a set schedule or plan. If they happened to be late for an appointment, it was okay because time didn't matter anymore.

Lucy's teacher, Miss Marino, had confronted Papa about bringing Lucy late for school. She looked at Papa disapprovingly over her cat-eye glasses. Papa was fond of Miss Marino, so he made sure to have Lucy on time for school after that. It was important to Lucy to earn a Perfect Attendance Certificate. Other than school, Papa didn't worry about being on time.

Papa and Lucy made up a lot of original songs and one of their favorites they co-wrote was called "Lago Time."

The lyrics went something like this:

Richard Rossi & Kelly Tabor

When Jerry quit the mill
He threw out his watch, and time stood still
Living on Lago Time
There's no clock on the wall
Time don't matter at all
We're living on Lago Time

Since Papa and Lucy liked Lucy's fourth grade teacher, Miss Marino, they wrote a verse about her:

When Miss Marino finished school
She ignored her clock, no more rules
She's Living on Lago Time
And it's feeling fine
Be still
Be chill
Come apart a while
It will make you smile
Living on Lago Time

Though they set out in the morning to look for Champ, because they were on Lago Time, they didn't make it. They got distracted sightseeing, having lunch at Captain Blye's, clothes shopping for Lucy, and trying to eat the Champ Monster Banana Split.

Truth be told, Papa was stalling for other reasons. He was afraid of losing Lucy the way he'd lost Lynn. "Lago Time" was a funny way to put off summoning the courage to look for the Lake Monster.

Yes, Lucy loved Champ, and Papa did, too. He knew the lake held uncertainty and danger in its deep, dark depths.

Chapter 8
Looking for Champ

Lucy and Papa had a bit of a stomach ache from the ice cream. They couldn't finish the Champ Monster Banana Split at Stewart's, but they set it as a goal to one day eat the whole thing, even if they had to get more friends to help.

Their plan had been to be on the lake by early afternoon, but being on Lago Time, they finally arrived later in the afternoon, guitar and backpack in hand. Days were longer in the summer, so they still had plenty of time to spot Champ before it got dark.

On their way walking to the lake, Lucy and Papa came to the Lake Champlain arching bridge that connected Crown Point, New York and Chimney Point, Vermont. Lucy looked up, up, up, past the top of the bridge to the sky.

"Hi God, it's me again," Lucy said. "Please tell Mama I love her and miss her. I'm looking for Champ like she would be."

Papa tilted his ear to the sky and nodded like he heard God tell him something. "What's that, Lord? Okay. I'll tell her."

Papa looked at Lucy with his sunburned, loving eyes. "Your Mama loves you, Lucy. She's so proud of you," he said.

Lucy smiled and her eyes clouded up. Then, she looked down from the sky and scanned the lake. It was silver-clear and statue-still. "Sometimes I miss her so much, I get knots in my stomach. I feel like I could just cry."

"Sometimes it's good to cry, and let the feelings out," Papa said.

Lucy & the Lake Monster

"When I come to the lake and think of Mama, and you, and Champ, I feel better, safe and happy, like I'm no longer sad and alone. It's like you're my guardian angels." Even though she hadn't seen him yet, Champ was more real to her than the child's world around her of school, classes, and video games.

"We feel alone sometimes, but you are not alone," Papa said. "I'm with you and God is with you. Always remember what the Good Book reminds us of, 'I will never leave thee or forsake thee. Lo, I am with you always.'"

"I'll remember that, Papa," Lucy said, smiling with relief. Papa had always been her fatherly figure.

When they finally got near the boggy shore of Lake Champlain, they walked down the hill on Bobcat Trail. True to its name, a big bobcat, twice the size of Bella, leaped across the path in front of them with its long legs and large paws. Papa stopped Lucy dead in her tracks so she wouldn't take another step closer to the wildcat until it was long gone.

When the coast was clear, they walked up the bank to their wooden, homemade rowboat. Some blue paint was peeling on it where Lucy had painted a drawing of Champ. Papa left the marking on it for sentimental reasons, cherishing her simple markings as he cherished her.

When Papa first saw their boat, which he'd built with his bare hands, he smiled like he was reuniting with an old friend. "Good ol skiff," he said.

Papa named it the "Research Vessel." He also had other names for the boat. Papa had christened it the "S.S. Champ Finder" one day, when he broke a bottle of root beer on the side of the boat. Papa had said it was "some kind of tradition." Lucy thought this was fun, funny, and a little odd, and she hated to see that root beer go to waste. His most affectionate name for the boat was "Ol' Skiff."

"You have our lunch, Lucy?"

"Yes, Papa. Yes, its in my backpack with my journal and phone. Aunt Joan packed us a couple sandwiches, potato chips, and apples from Gunnisons, remember?"

"Oh, yeah. I remember, Lucy." Papa helped Lucy put on her life jacket then put on his own. Papa double-checked to see if Lucy was fastened tightly. "Are you snapped in good?" Papa said.

Lucy nodded, "Yes."

"Good, because the Research Vessel can feel unsteady at times." Papa made sure Lucy sat in the middle of their little boat, not too close to the edge. "There, I want you to be balanced where you sit so we don't-"

"Flip over?"

"Yes, or fall out. I know you asked me if you could get baptized in the lake one day, but I don't want you to get baptized accidentally, Lucy." He giggled at the thought.

The sun beat down on their boat, so they were thankful they'd brought lemonade and waters with them to stay hydrated. Papa and Lucy sipped their lemonade, which tasted good under the hot rays.

They both wore hats for protection from sunburn. Papa wore his fisherman hat with a flag on the front. Lucy wore her Champ hat. Papa made sure Lucy put a bit of sunscreen on her pale skin so she wouldn't get sunburn.

Lucy & the Lake Monster

As they paddled out further, Papa saw the faces of fishermen and reporters on the shore. They laughed at Lucy and Papa's pilgrimage against insurmountable odds.

Lucy and Papa heard the D & H freight train in the distance, making its route down from Canada hauling plywood. It would pass Port Henry and make its trek down to Pennsylvania. Then, they heard the lake loons in the distance as they drifted with the current.

"I love it out here on the lake," Lucy said. 'I see the sun, and the trees, and the water is super clear."

"It's more clear than normal, like glass, which will give us a better chance at seeing him move," Papa said. "Normally, it's murky, because it's a clay-bottom lake."

Every time they went out on the Research Vessel, Papa had a ritual of packing lemonade and waters, sandwiches, hats, lifejackets, sunscreen, binoculars, and of course his guitar, because Papa believed Champ liked soft music.

Papa strummed his guitar and Lucy sang with him,

My sweet Lake Lady
We'll live on our boat upon the sea
You, Champ, and me...

After they finished singing, Papa played soft, instrumental music. He tapped his foot softly in contented rhythm.

"Keep playing soft, Papa. The music might draw Champ." He played the guitar for a while, then he thought of looking for Champ further out in the lake.

"Water's still nice and calm right now. I think I can move these oars and we'll get further out," Papa said. "Should we go left or right today?"

"I think Champ likes the left better today, Papa."

"Good. Let's go to the left today since we checked the right the last time." Papa felt a little pain in his chest and belly when he rowed the wooden oars. He'd had some surgeries that left scars over his belly and sides, but he and Lucy were determined to see Champ. "Maybe I'll let you oar a little bit today, Lucy. Let me teach you. Come right up here and sit beside me. I'll show you how to do it."

"Okay," Lucy said as she steadied herself to sit beside him.

"Now, when you pull the oars back, and both your hands are even like this," Papa said, demonstrating as he pulled the oars towards his chest, "you're gonna go straight back. If you pull just the right oar, the boat will go left, and vice-versa."

"Like this?" Lucy asked, imitating Papa's movements.

"Yeah. Let me get us a little further out, then I'll let you take a turn and do it. You can maneuver and get some practice."

"Okay. It's so nice to row further out on the lake, Papa."

"Yes, it is, honey. I've been coming out here since I was a little boy. Long before you or your Mama were even here."

"When you were a little boy, did you ever see Champ?"

"I looked and looked for him." Papa looked longingly at the lake. He watched a dark, double-crested cormorant dive into the water to catch a small fish. "Back then, we didn't have cell phones or internet. When people saw Champ, they weren't able to take a picture with a phone. News didn't spread as fast as it does now."

The double-crested cormorant came up from the lake holding the fish sideways, looking like a California surfer riding his surfboard, to make the fish more aerodynamic to carry. Then, it sliced into the wind, flying away to rest on a sugar maple tree limb and enjoy its catch.

"Had you heard stories about Champ when you were little, Papa?"

"I remember my grandpa telling me that one time, he and his friends were on their way to work one morning."

"Where did they work?"

"Up in the mines in Mineville. Grandpa said, when he and the other miners were headed toward Port Henry through the rock-cuts, where the lake is close to the road, they saw something unusual there in the water."

Lucy squirmed. "Champ?"

"That's what I thought. I remember asking my grandpa, 'Really? What did it look like?'"

"What did he say, Papa?"

"'At first,' he said, 'we thought it was an overturned rowboat, but it was kind of odd. It had a broad body. We weren't really sure, but the more we thought about it, the more we thought it could be the Lake Champlain Monster people talk about.' So, I think my grandpa saw it."

"Did *you* ever see it, Papa?"

Richard Rossi & Kelly Tabor

Lucy had asked Papa this many times, and he had told her the story many times, but he never grew weary of her asking. His story changed a little each time, and grew more dramatic with the telling, but the basic facts were the same.

"One time, I was out with some friends fishing, hoping to catch a big northern pike. There are also big lake sturgeons. Some people confuse Champ with sturgeons. Anyway, I saw something, and I could've sworn it was Champ because it was huge and it had humps."

"Your friends didn't believe, did they?" Lucy asked. She knew this from hearing the story before.

"My friends said, 'No, that's not Champ. That's just a big ol' lake sturgeon.'"

"I don't mean to be rude about your friends, but they were big dummies."

"Really?" Papa chuckled. "All because they didn't believe?"

"Yes, but you believe, don't you, Papa?"

"Deep down in my heart, I think it was Champ," Papa said, nodding. "I had better vision then. I could've sworn it was Champ. I remembered seeing the diagrams of Champ in Samuel de Champlain's diary. He was the man who discovered the lake, you know."

"I know. Miss Marino taught me about him. You've mentioned him before, Papa."

"What he sketched is what I saw, and what the Indians told him that they saw. So, I agree with you about those guys, Lucy. They didn't know what they were talking about, but I do know what I'm talking about. I believe it was Champ and you believe your Papa, don't you, Lucy-lu?" Papa smiled, and his face filled with light.

"Yes, I believe in you, Papa. I just wish you would've got a picture."

"Me too, but I've got a picture in my mind and in my memory." Papa pointed to his forehead. "I'm gonna have to practice with my camera, Lucy, so I can get fast pictures. When Champ appears, it's quick like I said, and then he's back under the water. He's up," Papa said, raising his hands, "and then he's gone." Papa lowered his hands. "You've got to have your camera ready when he's up there." Papa was right. He wasn't good with his cell phone camera. Talking about pictures reminded Papa to turn it on and have it ready. "I want to get a better view of Champ when we get the picture," Papa said. "Just like Sandra Mansi."

"Who was she?" Lucy asked.

"She took a picture of Champ in 1977, in St. Albans, Vermont, on her Instamatic camera. It's the one I showed you in the book."

"I LOVE that picture," Lucy said.

"Mrs. Mansi said Champ's head rose six feet out of the water, and twelve feet of his body was exposed. She watched him for a few minutes. He normally doesn't show himself that long."

Some of the residents of Bulwagga Bay who challenged them earlier at Captain Blye's shook their heads from the shore at Papa and Lucy. They stared at the solitary little boat as Lucy and Papa floated along, alone in their skiff. To the normies, they were an old man and his little granddaughter trying to find proof of Champ, something many people for many years with bigger boats and better equipment tried to do and failed. No one was able to get a good picture since Sandra Mansi in 1977, but Lucy was determined to get the next great legendary photo.

One of the people shaking his head in mockery was Sam the Scientist. "That old fool," Sam said aloud, his voice carrying across the water loud and clear to Lucy and Papa.

Beside him were the two writers for the local paper who wrote news articles making fun of Papa, Lynn, (Lucy's mother), and Lucy. Sometimes they wrote hurtful, outright lies about them. It seemed like bad news sold more than good news these days, and mean-spirited articles were more prevalent than goodwill. The first of the two writers, Roger Melnick was tall and skinny and the other writer Karl Kane, was short and heavy-set.

"Maybe while they're out looking for Champ, old man Lago and Lucy will spot some unicorns and fairies too," skinny Roger Melnick said from the shore.

"And they can capture the Easter Bunny, Santa, and a flying Spaghetti Monster," chubby Karl Kane said. Kane and Melnick laughed sarcastically, mocking Lucy and Papa.

Larry Lore, the third reporter, stood off by himself watching Papa and Lucy in their boat. "Hey, cool it you guys," Lore said to Kane and Melnick. "Have you ever for once thought about the trauma that family's been through? Go easy on them."

"That's why I'm an ace reporter and editor and you're not," Kane snapped back. "You pitch softball questions. I throw blazing fastballs."

Larry Lore shook his head, deciding not to answer a fool according to his folly. He ran his hand through his short, silver hair and smiled, hopeful Papa and Lucy might see something.

Papa saw the villagers on the shore, standing in the gritty sand. He answered their questions aloud, almost as if he read their minds, as he spoke to Lucy.

"We're really sincere, Lucy. Champ is looking for people who are sincere," Papa said. "A lot of people with bigger boats have tried to find him, but maybe they weren't as sincere as you and me."

Chapter 9
Camera Ready

The lake lapped against Lucy's skiff, then the waters grew choppier, beating against their beat-up boat, but they forged on, looking for Champ. Lucy looked at the Lake Champlain Bridge in the distance through her binoculars and remembered praying on the bridge earlier. Papa had told her most Champ sightings are near the bridge, at Bulwagga Bay. Lucy squinted to see further and saw Vermont.

She scanned the lake with her binoculars, looking towards Fort Crown Point, at the border of New York and Vermont. She remembered her teacher, Miss Marino, mentioning the Founding Fathers who visited there. Ben Franklin, George Washington, Thomas Jefferson, and James Madison all came to Fort Crown Point. She felt encouraged that history was made in that very spot, and she hoped she and Papa could make history by proving Champ's existence.

"Papa, I see something white, just above the water. It's moving fast. The waves are getting higher."

Papa oared closer, squinting. It was hard to tell what the stirring in the water was, because if it was Champ, he didn't surface above the water. "I think it's a seagull, Lucy. What do you think?"

As the S.S. Champfinder got closer, the white spot came into focus. "Oh, it's just a pair of ducks, Papa."

Lucy & the Lake Monster

Lucy's face fell forward, crestfallen, yet, she had faith and didn't give up. Papa laughed to lighten the mood. "Just a pair of ducks," he said. "We tried."

"Why did my hopes get so high, Papa? Then, it's just ducks?"

"During the Fall, canvasback ducks will be flying south because winter is around the bend. We'll see more and more ducks flying over then. When you see them making a V-formation in the sky, they're headed South where the weather is warmer. Let's keep on looking. Sorry for another false duck alarm, Lucy," Papa said with a chuckle.

"That's okay, Papa."

They paddled around the bay for some time. Once in a while, they were startled by a splash. It excited them for a moment until they realized it was just a fish.

"Why do the fish jump like that, Papa?" Lucy asked.

"Remember what I told you at Captain Blye's about that?"

"Yes, I saw a fish jump as I was using Uncle Bob's binoculars," Lucy said.

"Sometimes fish are predators going after smaller insects or minnows. They jump because they're hunting insects near the surface of the water. It's called feeding."

"Yes, Papa. That's reminds me of feeding fish in class. Miss Marino has an aquarium with lots of rainbow fish."

"The lake is one big aquarium. So, they jump out of the water to eat the bugs, making a splash."

"Oooh, gross," Lucy said.

"Ooooh, the food chain can be nasty sometimes, Lucy," Papa said, imitating Lucy's disgust. "Sometimes they're prey of other fish. They jump because other fish or birds are hunting them.

"If I was God, I would make a nicer food chain, Papa."

"How would you do that, Lucy?"

"We could all eat like the plants, through photosynthesis, making food through the sunlight, without killing someone."

"That would be nicer. You have great questions. I've wondered about that, too.

Speaking of eating, are you getting a little hungry yet, Lucy?"

"Yes."

"How about getting that peanut butter and jelly out?" Lucy reached for Aunt Joan's sandwiches. "Careful. Don't rock the boat, Lucy." Papa smiled at Lucy as she struggled to maintain her balance. "We don't want to tip over, do we?"

"No." She handed Papa a PB&J sandwich and took a bite of a Fluffernutter for herself. "Mmmm, these sandwiches are good, Papa. I wonder if Champ likes the smell of peanut butter? I think he probably does."

"You think so?"

"Yes. Hey, can I row now?"

"Please. I'm getting a little tired. I need your help, Lucy. Your old Papa needs a break. Some young blood is needed at the helm." Papa stood up slowly, wincing from pain in his legs that was like a celestial hand tapping him on the back, reminding him he was getting older.

Lucy & the Lake Monster

"Okay." Lucy was excited to take the oars for the first time. With Papa watching her closely, she oared out further.

"You're doing just fine, Lucy. You're a sailor, and I'm an old salt. Since Champ likes music, I'm gonna play my guitar real soft," Papa said, as he grabbed his guitar again. Lucy stopped oaring. He played arpeggios, picking each of the six strings one at a time. "Let me know if you see anything."

She squinted to see further ahead and saw a nice view of Vermont. She got a whiff of a strange odor. "Oooh, what's that smell, Papa?"

"That smell, Lucy, is good old cow manure, from the dairy farms of Vermont. Those clay-footers work hard, and I appreciate the milk they give us, but their cow manure gives off such a stink."

"Why do you call them clay-footers, Papa?"

"When you look across Lake Champlain from here, you see all the clay banks on the Vermont side. That's why we call them clay-footers. And when there's a strong east wind, look out New Yorkers, it's drifting our way, like it or not. The smell of cow poop is no respecter of persons. Keep your eyes and your ears open, Lucy."

"I will. But I'll keep my nose closed," Lucy said, pinching her nose and laughing. "P-U." Lucy rowed, then added, "But I appreciate the milk and cookies, and so does Santa on Christmas Eve."

Suddenly, she noticed something again. She looked through her binoculars. "I see a dark spot, way out there on the water," Lucy said, pointing. "Maybe it's Champ."

"Where?" Papa said.

Lucy pointed to the right. "There! Over by the bridge."

"Steer to the right, Lucy."

Lucy pulled on one oar to steer to what she saw. She oared like an expert who had been rowing boats for years.

"The waves are getting higher again." She looked through the binoculars.

"What is that?" Papa said.

"I think its Champ's tail making waves, Papa."

"Let's row out closer," Papa said. "Something is stirring in the water and the waves. Do you see it coming up, Lucy?"

"No, it went up and down too fast."

"Get the camera ready, Lucy."

"Start playing, start playing," Lucy said. "He likes the music." Papa strummed and hummed.

Lucy got jumpy, seeing something again. "It looks like a dinosaur head. Gosh. It looks like the head is rising up a little bit," Lucy said. "Moving to the rhythm of your music." She broke off a piece of her Fluffernutter and tossed it in the water, in case Champ was hungry.

"Yes, draw it in your journal, Lucy," Papa said.

Lucy made a quick sketch of what she saw. She drew a smile on Champ's face. "He doesn't look scary at all," Lucy said. "He looked like what I imagined when I dreamt about him. I wonder if that's what Mama saw?"

Lucy & the Lake Monster

"It may have been what your Mama saw," Papa said. As they approached the spot, they saw was a large piece of driftwood and broken branches tossed by wind and waves. "Sorry for the disappointment, Lucy."

"That's okay, Papa." She crossed her arms and looked down for a moment.

"There's an old saying, 'If at first you don't succeed, try, try again,'" Papa said.

"Ricky Taschner, the boy who likes me at school, he plays baseball. He made a joke about that saying. Wanna hear it?"

"Sure."

"If at first I don't succeed, I'll try playing second base," Lucy said. The joke jolted her out of her disappointment.

This pattern continued over and over. Every time they spotted something in the water, it turned out to be something other than Champ. The last letdown was when there was a disturbance and a hump sticking out of the water. When they rowed closer, it was a turtle tangled in a plastic bag. The turtle was exhausted, caught in the bag for days. Lucy and Papa were saddened by humans harming an innocent animal by their trash in the lake.

"It's a miracle it didn't drown," Papa said, as he cut the bag with his jackknife, setting the turtle free, before heading home. Lucy made sure she took the trash from the lake so it wouldn't harm another animal.

Lago Time had worked against them, because the late start gave them only a few hours of daylight. If they had spotted Champ, he hid as soon as they got too close.

As dinnertime rolled around, they got hungry again and ate some more of their sandwiches. Lucy liked the way the sun had melted the marshmallow crème into the peanut butter. Eating sandwiches was a way to avoid the feeling that once again, like so many other times, they didn't see Champ.

Papa's heart broke to see Lucy's disappointed face. "How do you feel, Lucy? We waited and waited for three hours."

"Well, a lot of people look on the lake for Champ and don't see him," she said, hoping to help Papa feel better if he was disappointed, too. "I know he's gonna appear one of these times. And we're just gonna keep on looking."

"I know we've been looking day after day. Long, hot days. It's been sweaty. Sometimes we come smelling good and we leave stinking."

Lucy chuckled and waved her hand back and forth under her nose like she was swatting away a stinky smell. "We stink like the clay-footers and their cow doo-doo," Lucy said, laughing even harder.

"Sometimes I stink so bad I want to jump off the side of the boat and swim to wash off," Papa said.

"Me too, but if Champ's under the boat when we jump off, we could scare him away, Papa."

Lucy and Papa were tired, calmed down like the lake itself. Lucy's eyes followed the faint yellow glow of the fading summer sun as daylight waned. Her ears followed the melody and intervals of Papa's voice as he spoke of his "Ol' Skiff" and the legends of the lake.

Lucy smiled. "The lake's my favorite place to be. I love being out on the water. Especially when it's nice and calm like this. It makes me think I'll be able to see Champ a lot easier because the water's smooth as glass. So, if there's any movement, we'll see him."

Lucy's eyes watched for any sign of Champ. She watched the iridescent beauty of a dragonfly as it skimmed across the water at sunset. Then, she saw some bats, who left the barn chimneys where they roosted to skim the surface for a drink at dusk.

The sunlight faded as the day was on the wane. Dark shades of night soon fell on Lake Champlain. Lucy turned on her flashlight and shone it on the teardrop silver lake one last time.

"See anything?"

"Nothing," Lucy said. Her disappointment was palpable. The sad lake fell below the lake-line watermarks on the shallow side.

"We'll see Champ one day, Lucy."

"We'll keep looking. I'm not quitting until I see him. There're many more days to come. We can try another day, Papa."

"Yes, Lucy. We can try again another day. Try/fail, try/fail, try/succeed. We're not gonna quit. Do you know what our last name, 'Lago' means?"

"No, Papa. I never really thought about it."

"It's an Italian word and it means something you're looking at."

"Boat?"

"No, it's not what we're sitting in, it's what we're floating on. It starts with an L, and it's not lunch."

"Lake?"

"Yes, Lago means "lake" in Italian. So, we are destined to find Champ in this lake."

Lucy smiled.

The lake was calm in its confidence that it held back its secrets. Like a poker player with a good hand, its face was stoic, not allowing anyone to name the time and place of its revelations.

"Maybe if we come out here more often, Papa. Especially in the evenings like this, when the water is peaceful. You can play your music again and maybe Champ will surface."

"Good idea, Lucy."

"Papa?"

"Yes?"

"Thanks for always taking good care of me since Mama's gone. You're the best person for me. You always look after me."

Papa was touched, deep down in his heart. He was at a loss for words, unable to answer for a moment. He took a bite of an apple. Lucy looked him in the eyes and smiled.

"I love you, Papa."

"I love you too, Lucy," Papa said, his eyes warm and shining.

The woeful walk home wearied their feet. An owl hooted overhead from the cavity of a white birch tree, leaving the egg clutch for a moment to hunt for its midnight meal. Lucy felt drip-drops of rain on her face before she and Papa made it back to their cabin.

Lucy & the Lake Monster

Before going to bed, Lucy opened her journal again. She got her favorite pencil out and wrote:

Dear Champ,

I was hoping to get a glimpse of you today. I just really wish I got to see you up close. Maybe next time.

I wanted a dog so bad, and it took a long time to get Bella. Then, I finally got her. Once I finally got Bella, I forgot about the long wait because I was so happy to have her. I think about the long wait once in a while, but I enjoy being with Bella so much that I don't really think about how long it took.

I WILL WAIT FOR YOU, CHAMP.

And when I finally do see you, I won't worry about how long I had to wait.

Thanks for always listening to me, too. Fourth grade is kind of fun, my teacher, Miss Marino is pretty and nice. She has frizzy hair and red glasses.

Miss Marino said all the great inventors, explorers, and scientists had the imagination to believe in things others don't.

Please let Mommy know I love her. I believe I will see her again one day, too.

The next time we look for you I hope we see you and I hope we can get a picture to prove you're real to everyone.

CHAMP, I LOVE YOU SO MUCH!

YOU'RE MY BEST FRIEND

Love,

Lucy

Lucy cuddled with Bella under her favorite blue blanket and fell asleep to the sound of rain on the roof. Little did she know the danger awaiting her at school the next day.

Chapter 10
Bullies

Lucy sat on the curb at the school playground, beside classmate Ricky Taschner, making simple drawings of Champ in her journal. Her friends played Hopscotch and Jump Rope nearby. Her drawings were based on her dreams of Champ and what other people said he looked like.

"I like your drawings," Ricky said. He brushed his long bangs out of his eyes with his hand.

"Thank you, Ricky. I never make Champ scary. I don't picture him as a scary creature. I picture him as my friend." She drew the outline of Champ's body with a black pen, then colored him with crayons, green for the body, blue for the lake, and yellow for the sun.

Suddenly, her Champ journal was snatched out of her hand. She gasped.

She looked up, up, up to the tallest boy, Butch Berrick, also known as Butch the Bully. He was held back several times from advancing to the next grade, so he was older and bigger than anyone else. He wore a tight, dark leather jacket and expensive silk shirts.

His favorite playground pastime was mocking Lucy and her faith in Champ. Butch told her she was silly and stupid to believe in Champ. He had another bully boy beside him who was short named Mousey McFarland. Mousey had dark hair, and dark weasel eyes, and a high, squeaky voice and echoed whatever Butch said.

Lucy & the Lake Monster

I feel anxious, Lucy thought, so she took a big belly breath.

Butch read from her diary in a mocking tone. "Champ, I love you so much," Butch said, reading Lucy's words in a high, girly voice. "So, you love Champ?"

"What's wrong with that, Butch?" Lucy said, standing to her feet with Ricky at her side. "Champ is awesome."

Then, he growled in his own low voice. "If you love Champ so much, why don't you marry him, Lucy?"

"Stop it!" Lucy said, as she tried unsuccessfully to grab her journal back because Butch held it too high.

"Lucy married Champ, so she's 'Mrs. Champ,'" Butch taunted, holding her book over her head. He led his bully buddy Mousey McFarland in a mocking chant, "Mrs. Champ, Mrs. Champ..."

Lucy put her hands on her hips. "Excuse me? That's not funny! It's not that kind of love, Butch. Girls don't marry sea serpents," Lucy said. "Besides, Champ lives mostly underwater and I can't hold my breath for a whole wedding ceremony. But if I could, maybe I would marry Champ."

Butch threw Lucy's journal down into a mud puddle. The bullies cackled while Lucy picked up her journal, which was now completely dirty, stained with mud. Some of the pages fell out when Butch threw it down. Knowing how much this hurt Lucy's feelings, Ricky instinctively collected the pages and handed them to Lucy.

"You got my book dirty, Butch," Lucy said.

"Everything about you is dirty and junky," Butch the bully said.

"Junky," Mousey McFarland echoed in his weasel voice.

"Your silly grandpa can barely breathe, and he's so old they're gonna take him away to the nursing home soon. And he has an old junky guitar, a junky cabin. That old, ugly, shack of yours is PATHETIC. Oh, and a junky boat that's so old it's one fishing trip away from sinking to the bottom of Lake Champlain," Butch said. "And he's got a white beard and his hair is darker than his white beard so he looks like a tire with whitewalls."

"Whitewalls, whitewalls," Mousey McFarland said. McFarland kept repeating "whitewalls" in his whistling, weasely voice. A few other followers of Butch passing by joined in the cruel chant.

"Stop making fun of my grandpa!" Lucy said, crossing her arms tight at her chest. "That is so rude. My grandpa works so hard and is so kind. How could you say that about him? Why do you have to be so mean? You don't even know my grandpa."

Lucy adored everything about Papa, no matter how old it was. She knew a man's value is not in what he owns, but in his heart.

"And you believe all the stupid stories about Champ," Butch said. "He's not real!"

"I believe in Champ," Lucy said. "Why don't you?"

"Because I have a brain and I don't believe insane junk like Champ or you," Butch said. "You probably still believe in Santa and the tooth fairy, don't you? No one's ever proved Champ. What makes you think a half-wit orphan and an old man are up for the job? And your mother didn't even stick around junky you or your junk."

Lucy & the Lake Monster

"Just stop it!" Lucy said, feeling like she could just SCREAM. She decided not to scream, worried it would attract attention and get her a trip to the principal's office.

"Just stop it," Butch said, imitating Lucy's voice in mockery.

"Stop it, Butch," Ricky said.

"Be quiet, Squirt," Butch said, picking Ricky up and holding him upside down.

"Let me go!" Ricky said.

Butch tossed him down like a rag doll. "Shut up, Squirt," Butch said.

"Yeah, shut up Squirt," Mousey McFarland echoed.

This last insult from Butch about her mother hit her right in the heart so hard, like someone punching her in the stomach and knocking the wind out of her. Lucy ran to Ricky to check if he was okay. He was a little dirty, but not hurt.

"The only thing junky around here is the trash that comes out of your mouth!" Lucy yelled at Butch.

She ran home crying, as Butch yelled sarcastically, "Bye, Lucy, have fun sea monster hunting with Grandpa. Change your shirt, it makes you look even poorer than you really are. "

She burst into Papa's cabin, closed the door and thought to herself, *I never want to go outside of our cabin again. I'll just stay inside with Papa where it's safe.*

Chapter 11
God Don't Make Junk

When Papa saw Lucy's tears, he asked what happened, but she didn't want to repeat Butch's hurtful words because she didn't want Papa hurt.

Papa was good at getting her to open up, so she finally decided to tell him some, but not all of the horrible things Butch said. The last thing Lucy would ever do is hurt Papa's feelings the way Butch hurt her feelings.

"This guy at school, Butch, he's not nice to me. He makes fun of me," Lucy said.

"I'm sorry, Lucy."

"He's really mean. And he's a lot bigger than me. He thinks because he's bigger than me, he can say mean, hurtful things."

"Like what?"

"Like, he laughs because I like Champ. He says if I love Champ I should marry him. I don't like it when he says stuff like that. And then he starts making fun of stuff I have. Things that we have, that are special to me."

"What does he say about our things?" Papa said, resting his chin in his hand.

Lucy answered slowly, still afraid of hurting Papa. "Well, he says that they're not new and shiny."

Lucy & the Lake Monster

Lucy didn't have to tell Papa the bullies called him and his stuff junk. He was smart enough to know what they said. He listened and observed everything around him. Papa was a wise old man.

Papa thought for a moment then decided he wanted to take Lucy on a field trip. "I want to take you to Walter's junkyard, okay?"

"Okay, Papa. But what does that have to do with Butch?"

"I want you to see how things that aren't new and shiny, that others think are junk, can be treasures. One man's trash is another man's treasure."

"What does that mean?" Lucy asked, as she held Papa's hand and walked with him towards Main Street.

"Do you remember when our neighbors, the Schlicks, set out that old Adirondack chair on the road by the trash can?"

"Yes."

"Well, one of our other neighbors, the Froehlichs, grabbed that chair and fixed it up for their house."

Lucy and Papa continued walking down Main Street until they arrived at Walter's Junkyard, a place with old cars, things people threw out, and several types of metals.

"There are things here that everyone else underestimates based on outward appearance," Papa said. "Butch may call my old guitar a junky guitar, but whose guitar sounds better, mine or his?"

"Yours, Papa. They don't practice, and you play all the time. Your 'junky' guitar does better," Lucy said, smiling. "You play better than Butch and his father. You make that guitar sing. Plus, that's the guitar Mama used to play when she was little."

"Yes, and that gives the guitar a sentimental value that is priceless. I've played it, your mother played it, so that guitar's been LOVED." Papa reached in his pocket and pulled out a guitar pick. "This was your Mama's favorite guitar pick. It's old and worn. I want you to have it."

Lucy looked at the pink-purple pick. It suddenly changed colors to the green color of Champ's skin.

"It's made from magic Alexandrite," Papa said. "It changes color depending on the light. At sunset it turns blue. At night it turns red. Your mother said it was magical. When Champ wanted to give her a message, it turned green."

"Does that mean Champ's talking to *me*, Papa?" Lucy asked, wide-eyed. "It turned green!"

"Yes, it's magical. The priests in the Old Testament wore a breastplate called the Urim and the Thummim. The gemstones in the breastplate would light up when God gave a message."

Lucy held the pick, staring at it in awe. The pick was worth all the gold on earth to Lucy.

"Mama will always be in my heart. And I will keep her dream going by still looking for Champ. The day I finally see him will be a special day. Maybe being called junk isn't that bad," Lucy said, smiling and pocketing the pick.

"That's right. A lot of great people have been called junk." Papa paused. "Do you know who Thomas Edison is?"

"Yes, Miss Marino said he was a great inventor."

Lucy & the Lake Monster

"Good, Lucy. I like your teacher."

"She's the best teacher in the whole world." Lucy already knew Papa liked Miss Marino by the way they looked at each other sometimes and smiled. "Edison invented the light bulb, Papa. Without him, we wouldn't have light to see things."

"Very good, Lucy. You're really smart. Thomas Edison said an inventor needs two things. First, a great imagination. And do you know what the second thing is?"

"What?"

"A pile of junk."

"Really? A pile of junk?" Lucy said, with her big eyes and smile shining. She looked around Walter's Junkyard at rows of wrecked cars and wondered who had driven them and how they ended up in the salvage yard.

"Yes, he had a lot of junk and metal at his laboratory. You and I have great imaginations and according to Butch, we have a pile of junk, so we're in good shape."

"Who cares about a bully's opinion anyway?" Lucy said.

"Man looks at the outward appearance, but God looks at the heart," Papa said, as he ran a hand over his beard. "You and I are somebody because God don't make junk." His eyes scanned the wreckage. "There's some real gems here. Some classic cars."

Lucy crawled into the driver seat of a 1967 white Plymouth Fury and pretended to drive it. Papa rode shotgun. "It's nice to drive you for a change, Papa."

"It's nice to be driven, Lucy. You're a good driver."

"You always make me feel better, Papa." They left the car and Lucy took a last look at the crushed and crooked metal parts and felt a kinship with them. She and Papa walked towards the exit of the junkyard.

Just as they were leaving, Lucy spotted a beat-up brown box. To others, it was ugly junk, but to Lucy it was the most beautiful box because she felt it needed her. She was intrigued by some stickers on the box that showed it had been places. The box was older, with stories to tell, like Papa.

It still has life in it, Lucy thought.

She looked closer at the stickers and saw they were travel stickers with the names of places: New York. Paris. Rome. She decided to make it her treasure box, then and there. The first thing she put in her box was Mama's Alexandrite guitar pick. Then, she added a silver and gold army eagle insignia pin from her father. He'd given it to her mother, and Papa gave it to Lucy after the accident. Lucy wanted to feel connected to her Dad too, even though he died in Afghanistan before she was born.

On the walk home, she found other things to put in her box. A white feather and a white stone that she found along the road were the next items to go into her new treasure box, after Mama's pick. They were the whitest feather and stone she'd ever seen.

Then, she found a blue marble. She put it in her treasure box because it was the color of Papa's blue eyes. She also added an acorn Papa picked up.

As evening shadows grew long, the fireflies lit the way, twinkling like stars, as Lucy and Papa walked the final stretch home. The fireflies sprang to life from the plentiful rain the night before.

Lucy & the Lake Monster

Like the fireflies, Lucy's eyes grew bright that night with the realization that what others judge as our greatest weaknesses, are sometimes our greatest strengths. Papa's words that "God doesn't make junk" brightened her heart like the fireflies brightened her path. Each one in their beauty shined brighter against the darkness of night, like Papa's words illuminated the way, overcoming the demonic darkness of Butch's bullying. Lucy knew that her and Papa were blessed beyond measure to be exactly who they were, and where they were, at that moment.

All the contents of her box were dear to Lucy's soul. These treasures healed some of the pain from Butch the Bully's verbal attacks and abuse. Nevertheless, there was one last thing she had to do, to stand up for herself. Lucy prayed for courage to do just that the next day.

Chapter 12
Legacy

Lucy was afraid to go to school the next day because of Butch the Bully. She walked into her fourth-grade classroom and saw her frizzy-haired teacher, Miss Marino, who wore a multi-colored granny dress, cowboy boots, and retro-red, cat-eye glasses. Several years earlier, she'd picked her first pair of red, cat-eye glasses and ever since she had a hard time choosing any other color.

Lucy turned to the right and put her coat and lunchbox in the seventh cubby box, which was hers and had her name on it. Miss Marino had twenty-two cubby boxes, one for each student. Lucy's cubby box contained pencils, Elmer's glue, crayons, markers, glue sticks, erasers, earbuds, and her favorite library book about Champ sightings with her homemade Champy bookmark.

Lucy went to her seat to unpack her book-bag. After turning in her homework, she wrote in her journal to settle her nerves. Then, she jotted a note to Miss Marino asking if they could talk in the hall. She discreetly slipped it on the teacher's desk as she went to the pencil sharpener. Then, Lucy told herself to breathe.

Breathe in, slowly through your nose, Lucy. Exhale. Out through your mouth.

Lucy used this technique to keep her anxious feelings at bay. She breathed like this when she was nervous, like before taking a test.

Lucy & the Lake Monster

Miss Marino looked over at Lucy and signalled for her to follow her into the hall. They quietly walked into the hall together as the rest of the class worked on their morning journal entries.

What is it, Lucy?" Miss Marino asked.

Lucy liked the colorful kaleidoscope pattern of Miss Marino's dress. She looked at the swirling colors, swallowed, and began to speak.

"It's Butch," Lucy said. Her voice was shaky and her lip quivered.

"What about Butch?"

"On the playground, at recess yesterday, he was mean."

"What did he do?"

"He bullied me. He threw my journal in the mud. He hurt my feelings and said, 'Champ's not real,'" (she said this part imitating Butch's irritating voice), "'and you and your grandfather are junk.'"

"Oh, I'm so sorry. I know how special your grandfather is to you. It hurts when someone says inappropriate things about the people we love."

"He even laughed, like it was a joke. But it's not funny. It really hurts," Lucy said, with pain in her eyes.

"It sure does hurt when people say those things. Who saw it?"

"Ricky Taschner was with me and helped me pick up my journal."

"What I'll do is I'll talk with Butch privately, okay?"

"Okay."

"Did anyone else bully you?"

"McFarland was with him, repeating everything Butch said."

"I'll talk to them both. I want you to know that you did the right thing by coming to me. Whatever mean things Butch said, disregard them. One thing to remember about bullies, is they are the one with a major problem, not you. So, I don't want you to take any of this personally. Sometimes people bully others to feel bigger and better by putting someone else down, because they aren't feeling good about themselves."

"He sure did put me down and make fun of me. He called me and my Papa stupid trash for believing in my friend Champ. And that everything I have is junky. And I don't understand why?"

"He's making fun of what you believe."

"Yes."

"How does it make you feel?"

Lucy looked down at the checkerboard pattern floor of the hallway. "Sad. But when I told Papa, he made me feel better by taking me to the junkyard."

"I'm glad your Papa helped you. It's good to have open communication with him, and with me as your teacher, because you can trust him, and you can trust me to keep you safe."

"Thank you, Miss Marino. That helps me feel better."

"There is absolutely NOTHING wrong with you and there is NOTHING wrong with your grandfather. And I also want you to know, if you want to believe in your heart in Champ, you should believe in Champ. What you believe very well could be real."

"Really?"

"Yes, really. There are a lot of people who claim they have seen Champ. Respectable people who wouldn't have been dishonest about it. Champ stories go back years and years ago when the lake was first discovered."

"Yes, Papa told me about that," Lucy said. "He has old books."

"I know you draw Champ in your notebook, so you're doing what the American Indians did, and what Samuel de Champlain did."

Lucy smiled, thinking about how important people in history drew Champ in their journals. "It makes me feel better thinking of other people who believed in Champ. Of course, my Papa does, too."

"And your mother who loved you so much. I was friends with your mom."

"Really?"

"Yes. She believed in Champ and researched about him. She went out on the lake trying to find him and get good pictures of him. She searched and searched and searched."

"Just like me," Lucy said,

"Yes, just like you," Miss Marino said. "You remind me of your Mama so much. Everyone in town remembers her and how she believed. Since she's been gone, you've taken over. And it's important that you want to carry on that belief and go for your dreams. You're carrying on her legacy."

"What does legacy mean?"

"Taking over where your Mama left off. You're going after the dream that she always dreamed of seeing. She would be really proud of you, Lucy."

"She would?" Lucy said, her big eyes shining.

"Yes. And I know your grandpa is proud of you, too. He loves you so much, doesn't he?"

"Yes."

"So, when these other people say things like this, putting you, your grandpa, and your mother down, I know it hurts."

"I felt crushed when they said that," Lucy said.

"If they ever do it again, let me know and I will put a stop to it because they shouldn't be treating you like that."

"Okay," Lucy said, nodding and feeling safer. "Do you think it's good I keep looking?"

"Yes, you love doing it. Don't let those boys beat you. You're gonna win. There are lots of animals that scientists are discovering in the depths of the oceans that they've never seen before. They're discovering new animals all the time."

"Like what?"

"There was a legend of a Japanese sea serpent they called Kraken. People mocked those who believed and they said it was cryptozoology fairy tales. Then, they discovered it was real. The Japanese Kraken Sea Serpent turned out to be a giant squid, with eyes the size of dinner plates. Someone filmed it in 2006 and proved it was real."

Lucy & the Lake Monster

Lucy's face lit up. "Papa and I are going to try and film Champ."

"Good for you. Don't give up or get discouraged. People doubted the Komodo Dragon existed until they found it in 1910. Same with many other creatures, like the tree kangaroo, the narwal sea unicorn, the platypus, and the mega-shark. They were all cryptid creatures thought to be legend that turned out to be true."

"What is a cryptid, Miss Marino?"

"A cryptid is an animal that has not been proven without a doubt to exist. Like Champ or Bigfoot. And many of them are myths that are never proven. But sometimes the myth becomes real because someone gets the proof," Miss Marino said. "Sometimes mythology and legend become history and science. So, I don't want you to doubt what you believe because of someone else's ignorance or how they're treating you."

"Thank you, Miss Marino."

"You're welcome." Miss Marino paused, touched her golden earring, then smiled. "Guess what?"

"What?"

"I'll tell you a little secret." Miss Marino crouched down to get on Lucy's level and moved her face close enough that Lucy could hear her speak softly. "I believe in Champ, too."

"Really?" Lucy smiled so big her face crinkled. Miss Marino smiled and brushed her crinkly hair out of her eyes. Lucy's smile morphed into a happy laugh.

"Yes. You and I have that in common, so we can talk about Champ anytime."

"Thank you. I will!" Lucy said.

"And don't you worry about Butch or his sidekick, Don McFarland. I will take care of them. It's wrong what they did. I'll even talk to the principal if I have to, to make sure it doesn't happen again."

"Okay."

"Because it's important that you feel safe at school."

"Thank you."

"Oh, you're welcome," Miss Marino said, smiling the warmest sunshine smile. "If you ever feel that you're in danger in any way, whether it's your feelings being hurt, or someone's picking on you, I always want you to feel comfortable coming to me and talking to me about it."

"I promise I'll tell you if Butch is ever mean to me again."

"Yes, and not only Butch, but if anyone else is mean to you, let me know."

"Thank you, Miss Marino."

"Now, I want the two boys to apologize to you."

"Miss Marino? I need to confess something."

"Yes?"

Lucy glanced over to the blue hallway lockers on her right and swallowed. "I said something hurtful to him to just make him go away. When Butch said those things, I told him that 'the only thing that's junky is the trash that comes out of your mouth.' After I said it, I thought to myself that I shouldn't lower myself to say hurtful things just because I was hurt. I don't want to hurt others."

"That's because you have a good heart, Lucy," she said. "Sometimes when someone says something hurtful to us, we react before we actually think about it. You were very upset at that moment and just wanted Butch to go away. I'm gonna talk to him and tell him to leave you alone because if he can't say something nice, he shouldn't say anything at all. And one last thing."

"Yes, Miss Marino?"

"Don't let those bullies change your mind. I'm really proud of you for believing in Champ." Miss Marino winked at Lucy and her golden earrings glowed again. "I hope you see him again, and I want to see Champ, too. And when your name is on the Bulwagga Bay sign, Butch will have to admit he's wrong because you saw Champ. Then, he'll probably be out there looking for himself."

Lucy hugged Miss Marino and they both laughed, happy they could talk about Champ and support each other's faith.

Lucy went from zero to hero in the eyes of the other kids when they saw Miss Marino supporting her claims about Champ.

Chapter 13
Take A Picture!

Summer days finally came. Lucy and Papa Jerry set out with the sun on their faces, boarding their beat-up boat they called the "Research Vessel" and "S. S. Champfinder" to look for Champ again. The faith and love in Lucy's heart for Champ was bigger than all the bigger boats in Bulwagga Bay.

"Champ is drawn to the sound of gentle music," Papa said. He said this almost every time before he played his guitar.

On the way out toward the bridge, Lucy and Papa Jerry sang "Row, Row, Row Your Boat" in a round for their first song. A Bohemian Waxwing flew overhead.

"Please sing our Champ song," Lucy said. "I love that song."

Papa strummed the Champ song for their second song, but he changed the words to mention Lucy.

"My sweet Lucy, we'll live on our boat upon the sea," Papa sang.

Lucy repeated the same lyric, putting Papa's name in the song. "My sweet Papa Jerry," Lucy sang. "We'll live on our boat upon the sea..."

Lucy and Papa both sang the next line together, singing, "Just, you, Champ, and me..."

The lonely lake was happy to see Lucy and Papa again. "I think Champ is deep, deep, down in the lake hearing our voices.

Lucy & the Lake Monster

It might sound a little muffled to him," Papa said. "He likes the sound of the guitar. Keep your eyes open, Lucy."

Papa was more correct than he realized. Champ was deep, deep down in the lake, touching the bottom of Lake Champlain with his tail. Champ liked looking up at the bottoms of boats and watching the schools of fish glide by like bouquets of flowers.

Papa's blue eyes got bigger and bigger as he scanned the lake from their Research Vessel.

He strummed his old beat-up guitar again on his beat-up boat then stopped. "Do you hear or see anything yet, Lucy?"

"No, not yet."

"We got to be patient. I'll keep playing."

"Play softly," Lucy whispered, "so Champ isn't scared away. Pick gently, Papa."

"Okay." Papa played his beat-up guitar softly.

"If Champ doesn't come now, something's wrong with him because that's really pretty music, especially with the sun setting. While you play, I'll look around to see if he pops up anywhere."

Deep down in the underwater caverns, the sounds of the song made its way into the sea homes. The underwater creatures were drawn to the music, beckoning the underwater animals to swim to the surface. Papa picked out some more chords, one string at a time.

After a while, they turned back, heading home, but still looking. They weren't too far from shore when they sensed something watching them.

Suddenly, Papa's eyes got so wide, Lucy knew he saw something. "I see something way out there, Lucy. Oh, my. Did you see that?" Papa said.

"What's that?" Lucy said, seeing a V-shape wake in the water of the lake coming straight at them. "Oh my gosh. I see something on the water, too, but I'm not sure what it is. Do you think it could be him, Papa?"

The water and wind-driven waves stirred again, revealing the creature. "I think so. Look out there to the left," Papa said, pointing with his finger. "I see something again. See that dark spot floating there? I can't tell if it's a log or if it's Champ, but I think it could be Champ, his snake part slithering. It's big, big as a whale and brownish-green." Papa strummed his guitar again. "Maybe he hears our music."

"Hopefully," Lucy said. Just then, a long, dark green tail moved through the water.

"Do you see it?"

"Yes, Papa. It looks like a big snake," Lucy said. Lucy got a glimpse of the long snaky body for just a half a second, moving in rhythm to Papa's song. "Champ," Lucy yelled as the long snaky tail came out of the water again and was much longer than they'd thought. Lucy was surprised to see him again so soon. "That was too long to be a snake. It was Champ!" Lucy smiled a humongous grin.

"Let's try to get our boat closer," Papa said.

Lucy saw Champ's massive tail swoosh for a second through the waves, and caught a glimpse of his girth, his whole body, shaped like a seal. It seemed to be about the size of a pony, but it was so quick, it was hard to be sure.

"Hurry up, Papa! Take a picture!"

Papa fumbled with his phone. He wasn't very good with cellphones. Just as he tried to take a picture a call came in, distracting him. "Do you know what I have to do to get a picture, Lucy?"

"Okay, unlock your phone, then, on the screen, go to the camera icon," Lucy said. A large, greenish-brown hump poked out from the calm surface of the lake.

"Camera?" Papa said, his fingers pushing the phone.

"Yes, press the camera."

"Okay, Lucy. Thanks." Papa was grateful Lucy was much more of a techie than he was.

"Click photo, then look out through it, seeing the lake." Lucy moved her hands, pantomiming what Papa should do. They were both so excited, their hands were shaking. "Press the white button," Lucy said, her fingers scrolling and pressing as if she had the phone.

"White button. Okay, Sunshine."

Papa was shaking and finally got to the white button. As he held up his phone, his hands shook like the weeping white pines on the lake shore shedding their needles. Papa and Lucy's mouths opened wide with wonder as they looked at Champ.

"His neck is so long," Lucy said.

They felt like jumping up and down in the boat but they didn't dare tip over the Research Vessel. Papa managed to get a photo of what looked like Champ's body.

Richard Rossi & Kelly Tabor

"I got it! I got it!" Papa yelled. Champ had turned and swam away into the darkness of the lake and was gone.

"I saw his long, green neck, it looked like a snake, Papa. I saw one of his flippers, just before he turned and swam away."

"Yeah, that's what I saw too, Lucy. It's good to test it off each other, to make sure that what we saw was what we saw." Papa nodded.

"Now maybe we can get our names on that sign in Port Henry," Lucy said.

Afterwards, in the wake, a large log floated towards them. "Now Champ's under the water again, but at least we saw him and got a picture, Lucy."

Papa and Lucy looked at the blurry photo. *Was it Champ's snaky body?* Papa wondered.

Lucy thought so. It did look like a log. Papa couldn't tell clearly if it was Champ's tail or the log. "I know I'm not the best photographer. But we're gonna keep trying and keep trying until we get the best picture of Champ ever, Lucy."

"It's okay, Papa. We'll see him another time, too."

On the way home, Lucy thought of people she'd seen that day on Lake Champlain. She wondered how they water-skied and rode sailboats so freely, without a care in the world, without a thought to the larger issue of the legend of the lake.

The two-hundred-year-old lighthouse across the lake started blinking in rhythm, flashing its red light. It was manned by mariners, signifying the coming night and guiding wayward boats. It towered above the lake and was a memorial to Samuel de Champlain.

Lucy & the Lake Monster

Before going to bed, Lucy opened her journal that contained pictures she drew of Champ and letters she had written to him. The journal still had some brown stains from Butch the Bully throwing it in the puddle at the playground, but Lucy had cleaned it up as best she could, with the help of Ricky Taschner.

She got her favorite pencil out and started writing:

Dear Champ,

Thanks for letting me finally see you today, Champ. Thank you that Miss Marino stood up for me when the other kids teased me about believing in you. And she told me to try again.

Love,

Lucy

Chapter 14
Naysayers

Lucy knew she had a real picture of Champ. She knew that he had caused the big log to glide through the lake with just a swish of his humongous tail. Unfortunately, when she showed the picture at a community picnic by the lake the next day, the doubters doubted.

"What you call Champ's tail in the picture was probably just the log itself," Sam the Scientist said, approaching the picnic table where Lucy, Papa, and Miss Marino ate potato salad and fried chicken.

"That's what *you* think. But we were actually there! It wasn't just a log, it was Champ's tail," Lucy said. "It was swimming, not just floating. We saw it slithering into the water."

"It was probably a duck," Sam said.

"Well, then it was a two-thousand-pound duck," Papa quipped. "And it was moving."

"It appeared to be moving because the wind was pushing the log across the lake. Logs become debris in the lake. Decomposition sets in, creating gases in the wood that make them appear more buoyant, like the log's swimming," Sam the Scientist said. "Then a seiche, a temporary disturbance in the lake's water level, propels them to the surface, making it look like an animal sticking his head out of the water, before descending to the depths. Plus, there's other problems with your picture. Nothing of scale is in your photo, like a boat or a building in the background that enables us to see how far away the object is and how big it is."

Papa meant well, but he wasn't good with a cell phone camera and his picture was further disputed among the townspeople. Some said it was Champ, some said it wasn't.

Lucy was determined to see Champ again, and if Papa needed her help with the camera, she would get a better picture of Champ herself.

"It's Champ," Lucy said, pleading for others to believe her.

"I'm humoring the girl," Sam the Scientist whispered skeptically to Papa. "It's just a wild goose chase. I don't mean to rob a child's faith, and sound like Scrooge saying there's no Santa Claus, but plesiosaurs went extinct sixty-six million years ago. The lake's only ten thousand years old. I say this as a trained paleontologist and zoologist."

"I don't mean to be disrespectful, sir, but what I just saw was not extinct," Lucy said. "It's alive and well. Prepare to change the science books."

"There's some very strange things in this lake," Papa Jerry said. "Very strange. Thank you for not wanting to rob her faith, but you risk doing that when you speak your strong objections directly to her. If you have anything too harsh to say, Sam, say it to me, not her."

"I can handle anything you throw at me," Lucy said to Sam, overhearing the conversation with Papa. "And whose to say all the plesyathingamajigs are gone?" Lucy said, butchering the pronunciation of "plesiosaur" as usual. Sam laughed.

"Lucy may not know all the big words and know how to say them just right, but she has more wisdom in her heart than all of you who mock her precious sunshine spirit," Papa said. "There's more treasures in her than in all your test tubes and textbooks."

"And she has the power of imagination. Just like Galileo, and Copernicus, and Isaac Newton. And Albert Einstein," Miss Marino said, chiming in.

"Maybe some of the plezy things are still around," Lucy said.

Papa showed Sam the Scientist another version of their picture of Champ Lucy edited on the phone, with a view zoomed in much closer. "In answer to your question about scale and how far out we were, we circled back toward shore, so we weren't too far out. It was shallow water."

"If that picture was taken in shallow water, only fifteen feet deep, the creature would be too large to come that close to shore," skeptical Sam said.

Papa Jerry rubbed his whiskers than answered the naysayer. "Sharks attack in shallow water. Some sea creatures come into shallow water."

Sam the skeptic was surprised Papa gave such a smart answer. He looked down on Papa because Papa hadn't been through as much schooling as the scientific critics of Champ. Sam had a doctorate degree in zoology, the study of the animal kingdom. He was an expert in evolution and ecosystems. The scientist didn't like being outsmarted by Papa, so his voice got louder and more argumentative.

"A plesiosaur's a lot bigger than a shark."

"If it's fully grown," Lucy said. "I have a good explanation for that, but are your ears willing to hear?"

"I'm listening," Sam said.

Lucy & the Lake Monster

"You're listening, but you're remaining skeptical," Miss Marino said.

"You say 'skeptical' like it's a bad thing," Sam said.

"Skeptical's fine, but you're beyond skeptical. You're cynical," Miss Marino said, peering at him through her red, cat-eye glasses.

"Okay, okay," Sam the Scientist said. "Let's hear little Lucy's explanation."

"Maybe he was an infant," Lucy said. "A younger version of Champ."

"An infant?" Sam asked, confused and outwitted by a nine-year-old girl. "What a bunch of nonsense."

Papa patted Lucy on the back. "You think of things, Lucy, that no one else thinks of. The American Indians were the first to witness Champ in the 1600's, so they have to have had offspring," Papa said, picking up on Lucy's point. "A smaller baby Champ could come into shallow water."

"Champ has a family," Lucy said. "In Burlington, and in Bulwagga Bay, many eyes have seen more than one come up out of the water at the same time. There's a younger one."

Sam spoke up, reiterating his disbelief. "Fables! Fiction! Anecdotal evidence not worth a plug nickel! Where's the evidence?"

"The evidence is here," Lucy said, holding up the picture on her phone. "We have a darn good picture here."

"Not good enough! Plesiosaurs have been extinct sixty-six million years," Sam said.

"Maybe it's not a plebio, plgeo, plebawhatchamacalit," Lucy said. She struggled to say the word "plesiosaur," but she knew if she kept trying, she'd get it right.

"You never answer Lucy's answers," Miss Marino said. "You just repeat the same thing over and over about plesiosaurs going extinct. You're a broken record, Sam."

Sam the Scientist did make this same argument over and over, almost every time Lucy saw him. And Lucy would argue back that Sam doesn't know for sure that Champ was a plesiosaur. They were like two chess players that repeated the same moves back and forth every game.

"You're just a Champ fanatic," Sam said to Lucy. Papa winced, and was ready to blast Sam for being cruel to Lucy, when Lucy answered herself.

"Why, that's a compliment," Lucy said, turning the negative energy positive.

"A compliment?" Sam said.

"Yes, because to me, f.a.n.a.t.i.c. stands for 'Friends And Neighbors All Trusting In Champ,'" Lucy said. "Right, Papa?"

"Right," Papa said as he looked away from the scientist. "Very clever, Lucy. How do you think of such things?" he said, chuckling. "Friends And Neighbors All Trusting In Champ."

Papa looked to Lake Champlain, shaking his head in amazement at how Lucy came up with words using the letters in "fanatic" as an acronym.

Suddenly, they all felt the wind blow, stronger than before at Bulwagga Bay. Papa Jerry looked back at the bullies and skeptics who mocked him and Lucy for believing.

"'The wind bloweth where it pleases,'" Papa said, "'and thou hearest the sound thereof, but canst not tell from whence it came or whither it goeth.' John, chapter three. Just like the wind blowing over Bulwagga Bay, we don't know how Champ comes and goes."

"I think about it a lot, Papa." Lucy said. "I wonder how he got here. I think of the Loch Ness Monster. He's been described by those who saw him as looking like Champ. And there's another one. It's out in the state of Oregon, in a lake out there. He looks the same, too."

"Folklore! Hoaxes! Wishful thinking!" Sam said. "It's just a way to draw interest to the economy of our struggling towns around Lake Champlain."

"You're supposed to be an open-minded scientist and you haven't heard a word I've said, "Lucy said. "It's not just in Lake Champlain, but in other places, too."

"Where?" Sam asked.

"Japan," Miss Marino said. "Something strange washed up on the shore and all the scientists were there trying to figure out what it was."

Lucy looked at Sam the Scientist. "Some of them used your favorite million-dollar word. They called it a 'ple-si-o-saur.'" She smiled with pride at pronouncing "plesiosaur" correctly.

"But that's impossible. Like I said, they've been extinct sixty-six million years."

"Extinct?" Lucy said.

"Gone," Sam said.

"Mister Sam, they're not all gone," Lucy said. "They're right here in this lake. There's a sign right up the road with dozens of names to prove it. Plus, a lot of scientists believe Lake Champlain was connected to the Atlantic Ocean."

"That doesn't explain why Champ is in Lake Champlain," Sam said.

Lucy sighed because she felt frustrated that Sam was so blinded to her side of the story. The Great Flood was an obvious explanation to her.

"In Noah's Great Flood, the waters were really deep and so Champ swam in parts of the world he never swam before." Lucy said.

Papa continued the explanation. "And when the waters receded, the animals landed in odd places, in pockets of water. Lakes in New York, Oregon, Florida, Scotland, where they reproduced. And some of those descendants are still alive today. And Champ is one of those."

"More mythology," Sam said, waving his hand. "And Noah and his family, eight zookeepers, took care of 14,000 animals," he said sarcastically. "They built a huge wooden ship, the size of the Titanic. How do eight unskilled people, Noah and his sons and wives do that?"

"Maybe God gave them superpowers," Lucy said. "Or maybe Noah hired some carpenters to help him build the ark, like Papa did. Papa built our log cabin."

"And Noah got all 14,000 animals on the ship and fed them all?" Sam said.

"No," Lucy said. "God brought them to the ark. And maybe they were young animals, so they took up less room and ate less."

"Never happened," Sam said.

"Lake Champlain could've been flooded by the ocean and then, it became an arm of the saltwater sea," Papa said. "Animals were marine migrants, free to come and go."

"And maybe the talking snake from the Garden of Eden gave Champ an apple to eat. Then, Champ swallowed Jonah who lived in his belly for three days," Sam said to Papa.

"You have no imagination," Papa said.

"Imagination? You two sure do have imagination," Sam scoffed. "And so do you, Miss Marino."

"Students with imagination are the best," Miss Marino said. "They're the reason I get up to go to work in the morning."

"I give her ten years," Sam said. "When she grows up, she'll think differently."

"You don't ever have to grow up if you don't want to, Lucy," Papa said with a warm smile, his hand on her shoulder. "That's enough, Sam," Papa said, strongly setting a boundary. "It's always fun to debate with you, but we're gonna have to agree to disagree. You know how important it was to Lucy's mother to look for Champ. And it's important to Lucy to keep looking for Champ, to continue that legacy. So, we're gonna keep on looking, and we're gonna keep on believing."

The scientist was silent, seeing Lucy's face looking like she was about to cry as she clutched her Champ figurine in one hand and her mother's guitar pick in the other. "I'll admit some sturgeon and salmon may have made it from the ocean to Lake Champlain, but as far as Champ, I'll believe it when I see it," he said softly, not wanting to provoke a full crying jag out of Lucy.

Lucy's mind drifted away from Sam. She comforted herself with a prayer and with some positive affirmations she thought to herself.

Lord help me, I miss my mother. I am still connected to her. I am brave, like she was. And I believe in Champ, like she did.

Lucy wished her mother could hold her. She knew her mother would understand how she felt like no one else could ever do. Miss Marino sensed Lucy needed consolation. She knelt down and hugged her.

"'Blessed are those who do not see, and still believe,'" Papa said to Sam. "If you only believe what you see, you miss out on a lot of important things. 'The things we see are temporal. The things we don't see are eternal.' Second Corinthians four, verse eighteen."

"Like what?" Sam asked. "What are the unseen, eternal things?"

"Love, and magic, and Spirit," Papa said. "If you only believe, all things are possible to the one who believes."

"It's the magic of believing," Lucy said, overcoming her urge to cry.

Papa and Lucy had a rhythm in which they would repeat certain things the same way each time. Whenever Papa said, "All things are possible," Lucy would always reply, "it's the magic of believing."

Papa turned to Lucy, their eyes making strong contact.

"There's magic in the lake, if you look in the right place...." Papa said, "...with the eyes of your heart. Don't worry, Lucy. 'Sometimes the foolish things are chosen to confound the wise.'"

Lucy & the Lake Monster

"'When I was a child, I thought as a child,'" Sam said, quoting back the Bible to Papa as Papa had done to him. "'I understood as a child. I spoke as a child. But when I became a man, I put away childish things.' First Corinthians, thirteen, verse eleven."

As Sam walked away, Papa strummed his guitar and sang:

My sweet lake lady
If you believe you will see
You, Champ, and me

Lucy and Miss Marino joined in the singing. Lucy felt peace as she gazed at the lake, and had a feeling her mother was there in spirit, singing along.

Chapter 15
Bad Guys

Beezel still got furious whenever she saw Lucy, because it reminded her of how Lucy's mother Lynn beat her out for head cheerleader in high school, and for captain of both the soccer and softball teams. Beezel wanted to be thought of as the number one Champ expert and researcher. But Lynn, and now Lucy, were nicknamed "Lake Lady," and like the title "Head Cheerleader," it was a title Beezel wanted to steal for herself.

Beezel, like Butch the Bully buying expensive guitars he never played, tried to buy her way into superiority over the Lagos. She spent more money than Papa saw in his lifetime, equipping her boat with giant nets intended to capture Champ, a metal submersion cage, fish-finder machines, underwater drones, and audio equipment. Beezel and Mike measured acoustics and echolocation, the sounds animals like whales and dolphins make and the echoes they listen for to navigate underwater paths.

One sunny summer Saturday, Lucy and Bella were playing at the lake with Lucy's green Champ toy. Papa was off in the distance, using his handyman skills, hammering on the front porch of the cabin. Mercenary Mike and Beezel Beemish snuck up to her.

"Where is Champ, Lago?" Mercenary Mike said, his voice hissing like a snake.

Lucy didn't answer. "Aaaah, aah," she stuttered, her mouth and eyes open wide. She was smart enough to know he didn't love Champ like she did, but she wasn't sure how to answer in a way that gave no answers. "I'm sorry, I just can't talk to strangers."

"We're not strangers, Toots," Beezel said. "We talked to you at the Champ float. I was friends with your mother."

"I caught wind that you saw Champ. Do you know where he is?" Mercenary Mike asked in a soft voice, his beady eyes shifting side to side.

"No. Not really."

"Point to where he is!" he commanded.

Lucy pointed to the lake in a general direction. As she looked to the lake, telepathically communicating the danger she was in, the winds howled, and the water levels lowered, trying to conceal their secrets from Mercenary and Beezel. "Where the water's wet. He's definitely there somewhere. Over there."

"Over there, Toots?" Beezel Beemish said.

"Yeah, somewhere," Lucy said. 'Somewhere in Lake Champlain."

Mercenary Mike strained his neck looking over the lake. The waters grew murky, stirring up its clay bottom to confuse him, and discourage any searching that day by him and Beezel. "I don't see him," Mike said.

Lucy's face was pale, with no expression. She stared at a hop hornbeam tree on the lakeshore for a moment and silently prayed for wisdom. Just then, a rough-legged hawk spread its broad wings and flew overhead. Lucy followed its path with her eyes to avoid looking at her nemeses, Mike and Beezel.

"Maybe you haven't looked hard enough," Lucy said.

Mercenary Mike was losing his temper, about to explode. "Beezel and I have looked for years, Lago. WHERE IN THE LAKE IS HE?"

"In the water."

Mercenary Mike grabbed Lucy's delicate face with his grimy hands. She started breathing fast and couldn't swallow. Her heart raced. She wanted to run, but told herself to be calm. Bella barked.

"I'm gonna ask you one last time. Where did you see him?" Mercenary Mike whispered, leaning in close.

"He's so deep in the lake you can't see him." (She said this to avoid giving Mercenary Mike and B.B. any real information, because she didn't trust them.)

"I'VE LOOKED DEEP IN THE LAKE!" Mike said.

"Sometimes he's invisible," Lucy said. "And he plays hide-and-seek." Beezel came over, beside Mike.

"This will be a goldmine for tourists," Mike whispered in B.B.'s ear.

"Especially if he's captured, Toots," Beezel whispered back to Mercenary Mike. Lucy had such good hearing, she knew exactly what they whispered.

Beezel knelt down close to Lucy. She was riddled with jealousy towards Lucy, and her mother, Lynn, but tried to cover it up. "Look, Toots. Your mother and I were best friends, so be a good girl, tell us what you know. And if you know anything your mother knew that can help find Champ, I'm all ears. If you tell me a secret, I'll tell you a secret. And you can ride in our cabin cruiser to get Champ. It's much nicer than your Papa's."

Lucy & the Lake Monster

"I don't think Champ should be captured. And Mama didn't either."

"This is worth a lot, Toots. All the candy you'd ever want. Especially if he's captured and-"

"NO! NEVER CAPTURE CHAMP!" Lucy yelled, cutting off Beezel in the middle of her sentence. "HE'S MY BEST FRIEND!"

Papa heard Lucy yelling as if she was in great danger. He noticed from a distance Beezel and Mike towering over her, as Lucy stood her ground. Mike noticed Papa and backed off from Lucy.

"Look, Toots," Beezel said. "Your mother, my best friend, had a camera before she died. Where was the film that was in that camera? I heard she got proof of Champ. She took a really good picture."

"I heard from my grandpa the film fell into the lake and was ruined," Lucy fibbed. She was honest and never lied, but she had to use her imagination to make up a story. "Yeah, that's it. The film fell into the water. It was never found."

Lucy did an excellent job of not letting Mercenary Mike and Beezel Beemish know too much. Papa walked quickly to rescue Lucy from the devilish duo.

It seemed like Beezel was always competing with Lynn. There were some confusing feelings and jealousies over Mercenary Mike who was in love with Lynn in high school. But Lynn wasn't interested in him. Beezel was in love with Mercenary Mike, so she was mad at Lynn for occupying a place in Mike's heart.

Richard Rossi & Kelly Tabor

When Beezel saw Lucy, it brought back a memory, unbidden, of how jealous Beezel Beemish was when Lucy's mother Lynn was crowned Prom Queen as the students sang their alma mater:

On the shores of ol' Lake Champlain
Nestled 'neath the pines
Stands our dear ol' alma mater
Pride of all our times
Truly we will always love thee
Faithful in our ways
And we'll never ever leave thee
'Til we end our days...

'Til the end of Lucy's days, she knew she would love and remember her mother. But Beezel was motivated by her hatred of Lynn Lago. Years later, after high school, when Lynn started Champ Day, Beezel started her Champalooza Festival across the street.

"Champ is a demon, a horrible monster," Mercenary Mike said.

"No he's not. He's NOT a monster, he's a hero! And he's my friend," Lucy said.

Papa was approaching closer. Lucy knew more than ever, he was right not to trust Mercenary Mike. And Lucy knew she and Papa would never give Mike another chance to lay a finger on her.

"Do you have any idea where in the lake that film might be?" Mike asked.

"*I won't tell him anything*," Lucy thought to herself. "No, not a clue."

Lucy & the Lake Monster

Papa grabbed her hand and they walked away. He turned to Mike and Beezel. "I try to be a peaceful and loving man, not a violent one," Papa said. "But when I see you two hulking over my little Lucy, who is so precious, I call her Sunshine, I feel like I could just go berserk. I'm controlling myself, but I've already lost one daughter and I'm not gonna lose another. So, if you two ever lay a hand on her again, I'll be the last lake monster you see. And it would be better for you to be in the bottom of that lake with a millstone tied around your neck."

Mercenary Mike nervously laughed, cackling at Lucy and Papa as they scurried away. Then, Papa looked at Mike and Beezel as they walked far enough away from them that their conversation was not heard.

"The people who are greedy, they say Champ is a monster to make money off people's fear," Papa said. "Just like some preachers do with God. They make God out to be a mean monster. Not all do, but some do. But God is good, and Champ is good. You know that in your heart, Lucy."

"Yes, I do, Papa."

"When people try to scare others, it's usually to make money off them."

"I don't trust people like that, Papa."

"I don't either, Sunshine. The people that accuse Champ of being a monster are monsters themselves. Champ's not a monster, Lucy. He's a creature God and Mother Nature made." Papa clutched Lucy's hand. "Come along with me, Lucy." They walked faster to get even further away from Mike and Beezel's evil energy. "I heard what they said. They just want money."

"They say Champ is a moneymaker, Papa."

"More people will want to stay here in Bulwagga Bay, because of Champ," Papa said. "So, there's some truth to that. But we have to hope that greedy souls don't turn Bulwagga Bay into some sort of Champland."

"What would they do, Papa?"

"There's a lot of things they might do. They'd catch Champ and eat him for dinner. Or they'd capture him. They'd make Champ do tricks, shows for profit for them and throw a few sardines to Champ. They'd wear him out. It's fun to have Champ Day, and Champ shirts, and Champ hot dogs. Nothing wrong with having fun like that. But, if Mercenary Mike and Beezel Beemish have their way, they'd sell Champ trinkets and hurt him bad."

"We can't let them, Papa. That would make me so sad. We can't let them harm my Champy in any way."

"No, we can't, Sunshine. God's greatest creations are meant to be admired. And if man's heart isn't pure like yours, Lucy, it's best he leaves Champ alone."

"How can we protect him, Papa?"

"People like Beemish and Mercenary Mike have always been around, Lucy. In 1873, P.T. Barnum, who owned a circus, offered a $50,000 reward for anyone who could capture Champ. Remember what I taught you before? In 1983, I helped pass laws to protect Champ, working with the Vermont House of Representatives and the New York State Senate. Champ is on the endangered species list. It's now against the law to harm him. The law said that Champ is to be free."

"I'm so glad, Papa. I want Champ to be free. I don't want anyone to catch him or make money off him. They should never do that to any animals. Especially rare ones."

Lucy & the Lake Monster

Bella barked in agreement at this as Papa said, "Amen."

"But some people, like Mercenary Mike and Beezel Beemish don't care. They'll break the law to capture him to make money for themselves. But don't worry. I didn't tell them anything, Papa. Because Champ is our friend."

Just then, there was an unexplained stirring in the water. Lucy gasped.

Chapter 16
Birthday

Papa threw a celebratory party for Lucy's tenth birthday on August 7th. He decorated his humble cabin with multi-colored balloons, garland, and streamers which hung from the ceiling.

Balloons also hung in clusters in the four corners of the room. Blue ones, yellow ones, red ones, white ones, and purple ones hung in a bundle. But most of all green ones, the color of Champ's garbage bag skin.

Lucy's favorite friends from school came. She was excited her friend Ricky was there. He had told Lucy he loved Champ and loved her. He was sitting on Lucy's left.

On her right were her friends, like freckle-faced Fiona in fuschia feathers, big-eyed Barb in a blue blouse, and laughing Laura in a lavender lace dress. They all wanted to be Lucy's friends from the first time they'd seen her at school. They were all so happy to be at her birthday party. Most importantly, they all believed in Champ, too. But none of them believed quite as much as Lucy did, and none of them looked for Champ as much as Lucy did.

Her friends all wore birthday party hats. Lucy had a special birthday princess tiara on her head and wore her Champ tee-shirt with a white hoop skirt with sparkles. Her yorkie Bella wore a tiara that spelled out "HAPPY BIRTHDAY."

"I'm glad my school friends are here," Lucy said to Papa. "But most of all, I'm glad you're here. You're the number one person I wanted to invite."

Lucy & the Lake Monster

"Awww, thank you Sunshine," Papa said.

Papa set out Champ plates, cups, and napkins on a Champ tablecloth. They had a scrumptious dinner of Lucy's favorites: mac and cheese, Champ dogs, and chicken nuggets. Lucy loved chicken nuggets so much, she said Champ had a "chicken nugget head." That may not have been the best description, but it was one that made Lucy smile.

Papa ordered the Champ Monster Banana Split from Stewart's Ice Cream Shop, but this time it wasn't just Papa and Lucy eating it, like the last time when they couldn't finish it.

"Are you ready for this?" Papa asked, as he carried the humongous Champ Banana Split to the table.

"Yeah!!!" the children cheered in unison. The entire birthday party participated. Each kid waited patiently for Papa to give them their share of the ice cream monster.

"I call the mint ice cream with little bits of chocolate in it," Lucy said. "Because it's green like Champ."

Papa scooped the mint chocolate ice cream out for Lucy and put it in her dish with a bright red cherry on top. "We're gonna finish it this time, Lucy. Ready, set, go!"

Ricky Taschner had his face so close to the ice cream as he scooped his spoon, that he got his face full of whipped cream. This made all the others laugh.

"There's no time limit," Papa said. "Enjoy!"

Freckle-faced Fiona took some dainty bites, but she concentrated on filming the proceedings so if they finished it, they could prove it to Stewart's Ice Cream. She gave herself this job because she was lactose intolerant.

Lucy, who always cared about others, worried Fiona felt tortured by watching others enjoy the ice cream. But Fiona said, "It's okay. I don't mind, Lucy." Lucy gave Fiona a special cupcake she'd made for her, so she wouldn't miss out entirely.

Big-eyed Barb and laughing Laura more than made up for Fiona's lack of participation. They scooped up the baseball-size scoops of ice cream, bananas, and whipped cream into their mouths nonstop until there were just a couple bites left.

"We did it, Papa!" Lucy said. "We finally accomplished our goal to finish off the ENTIRE Champ Monster Banana Split," Lucy said as she finished the last bite of mint chocolate chip ice cream. "Green ice cream. The color of Champ!"

Lucy was so proud of the group's accomplishment, that she didn't care about the ice cream on her chin. Her friends didn't care that they got a little messy, either. It was a marvelous kind of messy.

Miss Marino had made a Champ-shaped sugar cookie for every kid who was there. The cookies hung on strings above their heads.

Papa told all the children to put their hands behind their backs and eat the cookies that hung above them. He said the first one to finish their cookie would win a prize, and they had to finish it in under a minute's time. As Lucy and her friends furiously chomped Champ sugar cookies, Papa chanted:

MINUTE TO WIN IT!

MINUTE TO WIN IT!

MINUTE TO WIN IT!

Lucy & the Lake Monster

The first one to finish their cookie was Ricky Taschner, so he won the prize of a Champ sock puppet Papa and Lucy had made.

Before Lucy blew out the candles on her cake, Papa told her she had three wishes. "Birthday wishes have a lot of power to come true," he said.

"Ready?" Lucy asked, bending over the Champ birthday cake.

"Yeah. You can keep your birthday wishes a secret from everyone, including me."

"But I want to tell you, Papa."

"Okay, I'll keep it secret. Whisper it in my ear."

"If I whisper it in your ear, will it come true?"

"Yes, it will still come true."

"I want to keep it secret. But I think you know what it is, Papa. For my first wish," Lucy whispered to Papa, "I wish all the bullies like Butch and all the greedy people like Mercenary Mike and Beezel Beemish who want to capture Champ would stop." She twirled her hair between her fingers, for extra magic.

"Amen," Papa said.

"For my second wish, it's a really big wish."

"What is it?" Papa asked.

"I wish Mama were still alive," she whispered extra-soft. "And I want to see Mama again."

"Mama still alive?" Papa echoed softly. "Okay."

"And for my last wish, I want to see Champ again even longer, and be best friends with him."

"What did you wish, Lucy?" Ricky asked.

"She has to keep her wishes secret, so they come true," Papa said. "But Lucy you can have a fourth wish, one that's okay to tell everyone."

"Okay. For my fourth wish, may every day be a Champtastic day!" Lucy said. Her school friends clapped and cheered. Papa smiled.

"That's a great wish," Papa said. "If you only believe, all things are possible to the one who believes."

"It's the magic of believing," Lucy said.

Papa grabbed his guitar and led the children in singing Happy Birthday to Lucy and she blew out her candles. "I call the head!" Lucy said, so Papa cut the first piece of the cake, Champ's green cake head for the birthday girl. Then, he cut pieces and served the other children.

"Do you think your wish for a Champtastic day will come true, Lucy?" Little Ricky asked.

"I guarantee it," Papa said. "Her wish is gonna come true. Lucy ordered a Champtastic day, so one Champ coming up."

He left the room and got dressed up as Champ in a big green costume.

"Where did your grandpa go, Lucy?" little Ricky asked.

"Beats me," Lucy said. 'He's full of surprises. It's never a dull moment around here."

Lucy & the Lake Monster

"Errrr," Papa growled in his best plesiosaur voice, returning to the party room. He made more friendly growls as he moved his hands and legs like a plesiosaur. "How do you like my Champ costume?"

Lucy and her friends giggled and cheered. "I love it, Papa," Lucy said. Laughing Laura laughed the loudest. Big-eyed Barb looked up at Papa in wonder and freckled-faced Fiona clapped.

"Good, good," Papa said, smiling through his Champ mask.

"You're not scary." Lucy smiled, still twirling her hair between her fingers.

"I'm a friendly Champ, not a scary Champ," Papa said. "Time to play 'Pin the Tail On the Champ'!"

"That sounds fun!" Lucy said.

Papa taped up a big drawing of Champ on the wall. Lucy and her friends played "Pin the Tail on Champ, taking turns being blindfolded and trying to attach a paper tail Lucy made to the drawing of Champ on the wall.

When it was Ricky's turn, Lucy put the green Champ blindfold around his head, then put her hands on his arms and spun him around while the other kids laughed and cheered. Ricky was so dizzy he walked like Mister Brook from Captain Blye's tavern.

Ricky was lost and confused. He attached the tail far away from the Champ drawing on the wall. Everyone laughed about this, including Ricky. When Ricky laughed, he showed the gap in his mouth from his missing two front teeth.

Papa and Lucy always played lots of games. Papa knew games, songs, and dances, that no other grownups knew, and he and Lucy also could make up games on the spot.

For the next birthday party game, they played "Drip, Drop, Damp, You're Baptized By Champ." Papa and Lucy invented the game, getting the idea from the game "Duck, Duck, Goose" and modifying it. The way the game worked was Lucy and her friends sat in a circle in front of the cabin. Papa, dressed as Champ, was "It." Papa held a Dixie cup of water in his hand and walked around the circle, dripping a small amount of water on each child's head as he said, "Drip, Drop...Drip, Drop...Drip, Drop..."

Suddenly, Papa poured the entire cup of water on a child's head he picked to be "It," yelling, "DRIP, DROP, DAMP, YOU'RE BAPTIZED BY CHAMP!" He first did this to Lucy, the birthday girl. She was playing with her hair when Papa doused her. Lucy chased Papa, trying to tag him before he sat in her spot. Lucy tagged Papa, making him "It" for another round.

All the kids had worn clothes they didn't mind getting wet because Papa and Lucy told them in advance about their "Drip, Drop, Damp, You're Baptized By Champ" game. After the game, Papa gave everyone a little washrag to wipe water off themselves.

Wiping the water away after "Drip, Drop, Damp, You're Baptized By Champ," didn't really matter all that much, because after the game, Lucy and her friends had a wonderful time swimming in Lake Champlain. After swimming a bit, Lucy threw a stick in the lake. She watched the stick float. Bella went in the water to retrieve it. Bella loved the game so much, they did it over and over. It was Lucy's best birthday ever.

Chapter 17
Baptism

Playing the game, "Drip, Drop Damp, You're Baptized By Champ" reminded Lucy of her idea to get baptized for real in Lake Champlain. She wanted her baptism to not be in a manmade baptistry at a church building, but in the watery grave of her Mama, to help wash away her grief, and heal the part of her that still felt dead inside.

Some of her friends like Ricky were baptized when they were babies. She hadn't had a chance to be baptized yet, but she felt that she was closer to her calling now than ever, and she was going to find Champ and fulfill her destiny. She heard Pastor Crowder talk about baptism, how Jesus did it to fulfill His destiny and begin His three year ministry. Lucy wanted to be baptized as a commitment, a meaningful moment that would change things. She found herself talking to God more than ever lately. Her prayers usually started with, "Hey God, it's me, your friend, Lucy. I want to get baptized in the lake."

After all, she thought, *Jesus Himself was baptized in the Jordan River.* She remembered when Jesus was baptized, a voice spoke from Heaven; and the Spirit, like a dove descended upon Him. The Heavens opened to Jesus. She hoped the Heavens would open for her, and give her a whole new understanding of things like Champ, and love, and magic.

After the party, Lucy brought it up to Papa and he reacted positively to her idea. Papa always reacted positively to all her ideas.

Lucy & the Lake Monster

"That's really nice you want to get baptized, Lucy," Papa said, as he cleaned up from the party, throwing paper birthday plates in the trash. "So how do you feel about getting baptized in the lake?"

Lucy bounced up and down in her chair. "A little excited and a little nervous."

Papa rubbed his beard then rested his chin in his hand. "What are you nervous about?"

"A couple things. The lake might be really cold, for one thing," Lucy said, then she laughed.

"Yeah," Papa said.

"But I like the outdoors. And Mama liked the outdoors. She spent a lot of time at the lake. I got to thinking, I really miss Mama a lot." She did her Lucy look, gazing up to her right, deep in thought. "I like to do things that remind me of her."

"Preacher Crowder said in a sermon that baptism is a burial of the pains of the past, and a rising up out of the waters to new life," Papa said, taking down a few birthday balloons that deflated.

"Rising to new life means we have to keep going, even though Mama's gone," Lucy said. "And face every new day."

"That's right, Lucy." Papa paused, then remembered Lucy said she was nervous about a couple things. "What else are you nervous about?"

"I'm also nervous about what type of miracle might happen," Lucy said. "If miracles still happen now and then, maybe Mother will rise out of the waters in the lake and be there in spirit form at my baptism.

Maybe God will allow her to be with me at this special time, Lucy thought.

"Miracles still happen now and then," Papa said. "If they happened all the time, they wouldn't be special and extraordinary, they'd be ordinary. But this is a special occasion. It's not every day there's a baptism in Lake Champlain."

"I wonder if anyone else got baptized in the lake?" Lucy asked.

"In the Bible they got baptized in real bodies of water, like Jesus in the River Jordan."

"That's what I was just thinking," Lucy said. "Sometimes you say the exact thing I'm thinking Papa. That's the Holy Spirit."

"Great minds think alike," Papa said, with a sparkle in his eyes.

"We don't have the River Jordan near us, but we have something better, the home of Champ. So, why not use Lake Champlain?"

"That's a great idea, Lucy. At the church in Port Henry they baptize inside in a baptistry tub. Although one time we had to have a baptism at the lake instead because Big John Verceranack was too fat for fitting in the..."

Lucy laughed and looked at some of her birthday cards on the table in the middle of their log cabin.

"...baptistry. He was 350 pounds and he was twice the size of the sacred tub at the church. So, we had to go to the lake."

Lucy chuckled again at this. "Was that the last time they baptized at the lake?"

"Yes, twenty years ago. You're the second lake baptism that I know of."

"Cool. It's the best time of year to do it too, because the water's warm, Papa. And who knows? Maybe Champ will show up for the occasion."

"Maybe he'll be an eyewitness," Papa said, grinning. "The way John the Baptist was an eyewitness to Jesus's baptism."

Lucy opened Papa's Bible and read a verse from the third chapter of John:

> *Jesus answered, Verily, verily, I say unto thee,*
> *Except a man be born of water and of the Spirit,*
> *he cannot enter into the kingdom of God.*

Lucy believed.

Papa had faith and believed, but deep down in his heart, he disagreed with God on some things. Papa loved Lucy so much, that if he was God, he would make her childhood much longer, so she wouldn't have to grow up too fast and find out how the world can be so unfair and mean sometimes. The second thing Papa would change if he was God, was that he would make pets lives as long as human lives.

If this were true, Lucy could keep Bella as her pet for her entire life, Papa thought to himself.

The following Sunday, after morning service, the parishioners of Port Henry Community Church gathered at Sandy Beach in Bulwagga Bay for Lucy's baptism.

Pastor Crowder asked Lucy to speak before her baptism, giving a public testimony to those gathered at Lake Champlain. Lucy stood before her teacher, Miss Marino, some of her school friends, and members of the church. Some of the kids sat on the shore, like Ricky Taschner, who shielded his eyes with his hands to block out the sun to see Lucy. Adults and older teens stood.

"I know there is a Power greater than myself," Lucy said. "God watches over me. And my Papa does, too. I believe Champ is in this lake, too. I don't understand everything that's happened in my life. Like why my parents are gone. But if God were small enough for me to understand, He wouldn't be big enough for me to trust."

Lucy's friends clapped loudly. She walked to the lake and Pastor Crowder took her left hand and led her into the water. Papa Jerry followed her and took her right hand. They walked slowly through the water feeling the lake's murky bottom with their feet.

With Papa on one side, and Pastor Crowder on the other, Lucy was immersed backwards into the lake. When they lifted her back up, the crowd on the shore cheered and clapped so loud it was heard across the lake. Lucy wiped the water out of her eyes.

Coming up out of the lake, she heard the seagulls cry and Preacher Crowder say, "In the name of the Father, and of the Son, and of the Holy Spirit. Lucy, you are risen to new life, rising out of the water. New, true revelations will come to you now."

Pastor Crowder's smile shone like the sun above. Lucy jumped up and down in the lake. "I'm so happy," Lucy said, crying tears of joy. "Now I have Champ's water with me, so I can go out and find him like never before! Thank you, Jesus."

"Yes, yes!" Papa said, hugging her.

"Hallelujah!" Miss Marino called from the sandy shore. "Hallelujah! Yay, Lucy!"

Bella barked an "Amen," then chased a squirrel up a large shagbark hickory tree.

Just then, Lucy felt an inspiration and a revelation. She heard a jet fly above through the summer sky. Lucy stared at the long, white jet stream and for just a moment, it split into different parts, forming three giant C's.

C. C. C.

What could this mean? Lucy wondered to herself.

Chapter 18
Champ Chomp Chum

Lucy's baptism went well. She felt closer to Champ and to Mama now that she was baptized in the waters of Lake Champlain.

Papa and Lucy felt they were very close to attracting Champ to their Research Vessel. They already knew Champ liked Papa's guitar music. When he played, there were stirrings in the water, as if something was right under the surface. Even the seagulls sensed it, flying above their boat. The songbirds sang from their nest along the shores. The lake loons eerie calls echoed the hoots of the barred owls.

Lucy and Papa were searching and searching for something else to lure Champ.   Lucy was fiddling in the kitchen when an idea struck her like lightning, the interpretation of what "C.C.C." meant.

"Papa, I got this great idea to attract Champ!" She was smiling and her little body was moving around in all directions as she spoke excitedly.

"What's your idea, Lucy?"

"A special recipe I make up myself." Her big blue eyes sparkled.

"Really? And what is the recipe for?"

"To attract Champ to our boat," Lucy said.

"Great. We can give some to Champ to eat the next time we go out on our Research Vessel."

Like Thomas Edison inventing the light bulb, Lucy invented Champ Chomp Chum or C.C.C. for short. Lucy remembered Miss Marino saying they used shark chum, a type of food to attract sharks. This gave Lucy an idea of dreaming up Champ Chum.

Lucy figured if she could invent the right recipe for Champ Chum, it might be the trick to finally lure Champ and see him long enough to get a picture to prove he was real.

"Champ will chomp the Champ Chum I make with his big teeth, so I call it Champ *Chomp* Chum," Lucy said, making chomping motions with her fingers as she laughed. "It's hard to say it fast. Champ Chomp Chum. Say it three times fast, Papa." Lucy looked up at Papa, waiting for him to try the tongue twister.

"Champ Chomp, Chum, Champ Chomp, Chum, Champ Chomp, Chum," Papa said, almost twisting the words.

Lucy wanted to make Champ Chomp Chum out of food in the refrigerator. Since she learned about shark chum in school from Miss Marino, she asked Papa if she could invite her to help her with the C.C.C. recipe. Papa loved the idea.

"That's a good idea," Papa said, with a twinkle in his eye.

When Miss Marino arrived at their cabin, Papa turned redder than a beet when she greeted him. She had been around Papa and Lucy in public places, like school and community picnics, but this was different. It felt like they had a famous celebrity visiting them at home.

"Miss Marino, I'm really glad, I mean *we're* really glad you came to visit. You're the best teacher Lucy ever had," Papa said.

"Why thank you," Miss Marino said. "Thank you so much for inviting me over this afternoon to be with you and Lucy."

"You're welcome," Papa said.

"Why, hello Lucy," Miss Marino said. "How are you?"

"I'm doing great," Lucy responded.

"Lucy's such a good student in school and a pleasure to have around," Miss Marino said to Papa.

"Yes, she is," Papa said, as he took a sip of coffee.

"I know Lucy calls you Papa or Papa Jerry. How would you like me to refer to you?"

Miss Marino smiled at Papa. He looked down to the floor of their cabin. "My close friends call me Jerry, and I hope you and I will be friends."

"Okay, Jerry," Miss Marino said with a smile. "Do you mind if I look around in your refrigerator?"

"Help yourself," Papa said.

"I love to cook, and I know Lucy likes to make concoctions in the kitchen, too," Miss Marino said.

"I sure do," Lucy chimed in.

"Lucy's very creative," Papa said. "Sometimes when we don't have a plan of what to eat, Lucy will take our leftovers and create her own dishes by mixing different things."

"I don't need a recipe," Lucy said.

"I'm excited to invent our own recipe together today, Lucy," Miss Marino added.

"I do think I owe you an apology, Miss Marino," Papa said.

"Yes, Jerry?"

"Since I quit the mill, I threw out my watch. I don't worry about time. I know I've had Lucy late for school a few times. I don't worry about schedules and appointments, but I don't want it to interfere with Lucy's goal for perfect attendance. Being late was disrespectful to you as a teacher. At least with school, I will think about the clock and get Lucy there on time."

"Thank you very much," Miss Marino said. "I appreciate that. You apologized before and I accept your apologies. Being on time is important." Miss Marino grinned, finding Papa's old-fashioned apology endearing and classy.

"Feel free to help yourself to anything in our kitchen, Miss Marino, for you and Lucy to make this Champ Chomp Chum," Papa said, leaving the kitchen. He sat in his favorite comfy easy chair and read his newspaper. "My fridge is your fridge," he called out from the adjacent room, with a twinkle in his eye.

"I love the name Champ Chomp Chum," Miss Marino said, smiling.

Lucy told Miss Marino she didn't believe Mercenary Mike and Beezel's sharp-toothed Champ statue was accurate, because she thought Champ would not eat other creatures.

"All right, Lucy. Since we believe Champ is a herbivore, he likes to eat plants," Miss Marino said. "Champ gets hungry. We don't want to catch him, we just want to get him to come really close to our boat."

"Yes, we don't want to catch and eat him like Mercenary Mike would," Lucy said. "If Mike and Beemish were doing this, they'd put fishhooks in the chum to catch Champ, but we won't. We want to see him and take a picture. He's our friend."

"Let's look for something plant-based Champ might like," Miss Marino said, as she and Lucy opened the door and scoured the refrigerator. "Something that might float, a veggie that's easy to carry?"

"All I see is some grape jelly, some meatloaf, and ooh, I found some celery," Lucy exclaimed, squirming her head and body to scan every crevice of the fridge. "And a little lettuce. Oh, and I see some carrots."

"Good, they are plants and will float, too," Miss Marino said. "What else do you think we could put with the celery, carrots, and lettuce, if we do it in little bite-size pieces?"

"Maybe we should add a garnish or something," Lucy said.

"Garbage?" Miss Marino said, mishearing.

"No, GARNISH," Lucy said. Her and Miss Marino laughed at the misunderstanding.

"We're having fun in the kitchen," Miss Marino said. Papa looked over from his chair where he was reading the newspaper. He smiled at his two favorite girls. He enjoyed the laughter coming from the kitchen.

"Have fun and help yourself to anything you find," Papa said. Miss Marino smiled at Papa and he turned red again, returning to reading the paper.

"So, some kind of garnish. We need something that will stick so it doesn't float away in the water," Miss Marino said.

Lucy & the Lake Monster

"Maybe we could put some peanut butter on it," Lucy said, demonstrating with her hands how to mix the two. "I know what Champ likes. He likes peanut butter. I've never heard of a lake monster having peanut allergies." She chuckled with Miss Marino, which warmed Papa's heart again. Lucy's teacher was a type of therapy in the absence of her mother, a type of mother-figure who filled a void. Papa saw that it was good, very good.

"Peanut butter! Perfect! That's what I was thinking," Papa said from the adjacent room. "Yummy! If Champ doesn't eat it, I will." This made Miss Marino and Lucy chuckle. "I might sneak a bite when you two aren't looking."

"It could be our snack on the Research Vessel," Lucy said, adding to Papa's joke.

"Peanut butter, lettuce, celery sounds good," Miss Marino said. "What animal wouldn't like peanut butter?"

"I found some corn, too," Lucy said, "and some spinach. Spinach looks like seaweed, so Champ will like that."

Miss Marino didn't want Lucy handling the knife, so she cut the celery and carrots into small, bite-size pieces, about two inches, and cut the corn kernels off the cobs.

Lucy saw iceberg lettuce and mixed lettuce in the refrigerator. She chose the mixed lettuce because she'd heard it was more nutritional. Lucy also figured mixed lettuce contained several kinds of lettuce, so if Champ didn't like one kind, he could try the other.

"How are we gonna ball everything up, so it sticks together?" Miss Marino asked.

"Oooh, I have an idea," Lucy said.

Lucy wrapped some of the small pieces of veggies in the mixed lettuce, then grabbed a jar of peanut butter in Papa's pantry cabinet. She put a dab of peanut butter on the outside and inside of the lettuce to help things stick. Then, Lucy mixed it all together in a bowl. Next, she scooped a spoonful of peanut butter to help everything fuse together even more. She rolled the celery, corn, carrots, lettuce, spinach, and peanut butter into balls in her hands.

"You can put peanut butter on top of the veggies, or the veggies on top of the peanut butter," Lucy said. "Either way it works just fine."

"Good job," Miss Marino said.

"Let's put a cherry on top for a garnish, just like the Champ Monster banana split," Lucy said, adding a red cherry on each ball. "The cherry's something sweet for Champ, like a dessert." Lucy laughed, looking at how her hands were messy from putting the squishy C.C.C. balls together, but it was well worth it. "Ooh, I see something else sweet that will help the C.C.C. balls stick together," she said, spotting a jar of honey and a jar of Marshmallow Fluff Creme.

"Good, Lucy," Miss Marino said. "Honey's something that could be part of his dessert, too, and it's something natural."

"And Marshmallow Fluff Crème can be used to make Rice Krispies Treats or Fluffernutter Sandwiches," Lucy said. "Tasty treats, and with healthy vegetables for Champ. Champ, Chomp, Chum!"

"Champ, Chomp, Chum," Miss Marino said, but not as fast as Lucy was able to say it.

Lucy and Miss Marino each made twenty C.C.C. balls. Bella barked, thrilled to be the canine vacuum cleaner and eat some scraps that fell on the floor. Lucy poured honey and Marshmallow Fluff Creme on the top of each ball, making one extra for Bella. When all the balls were done, they put them on wax paper on top of a cookie sheet, then slid it into the refrigerator for ten minutes to harden.

The ten minutes took a long time. Each tick-tock of the clock seemed slow. "Why does time go slower when you watch the clock and are waiting for something?" Lucy asked.

"Albert Einstein taught us that time is relative and different things can make it appear to pass fast or slow," Miss Marino said. "Like summer vacation seems to go by so fast, doesn't it?"

"Yes, Miss Marino," Lucy said.

After the ten minutes, the balls were done. "I wonder if these Champ Chomp Chum balls will float?" Lucy asked.

"We'll have to test them," Miss Marino said. "Remember in science class we learned about the Scientific Method?"

"Yes," Lucy said. "Experiment to test your hypothesis."

"Very good," Miss Marino said as she filled the sink with water.

"Because if they don't float, we won't see Champ," Lucy said.

"Yes, because if the Champ Chomp Chum sinks underwater, you wouldn't see Champ unless you swam under water snorkeling," Miss Marino said.

"We want Champ to come to the surface," Lucy said. "Let's test the floating hypothesis!"

"Good idea," Papa said, joining them for the test.

146

"Its fun being scientists," Lucy said, laughing. "And to test it out, let's throw in some magic. We have to all say the magic words, 'Champ, Chomp, Chum' three times in a row."

They put a Champ Chomp Chum ball in the sink full of water for the test. Together, in unison, the three of them said:

CHAMP, CHOMP, CHUM!

CHAMP, CHOMP, CHUM!

CHAMP, CHOMP, CHUM!

It was hard to say it three times fast. Lucy did it easily, but Miss Marino struggled with the words a bit and laughed. They were truly magic words, for magic and love were in the C.C.C. balls that had extra enchantment to draw Champ to the surface of the lake.

"You are the Official Scientist of the day," Miss Marino said. "So you are the tester, Lucy."

Lucy dropped a C.C.C. ball in the water. "They float!" Lucy said, smiling. Miss Marino's mouth was wide open in wonder. "Champ's gonna be chomping chum!" Lucy said.

"Perfect!" Miss Marino said. "I love it! The next time you and Papa go out on the boat, you can bring some of this and toss some in the water."

"And when the sun's going down, Papa can play his guitar," Lucy said. "Champ likes Papa's peaceful music. Hopefully, he'll come to the surface, and I'll throw some chum in the water, and Champ will eat them."

"Good idea, Lucy," Miss Marino said. "You should throw the balls in the lake because you've got a great arm like a baseball player. I've watched you playing catch with Ricky Taschner on the playground."

"He taught me how to throw a baseball real good." She pantomimed throwing.

"Real *well*," Miss Marino said, correcting Lucy's grammar. "You're gonna get lots of practice throwing the chum. Champ is big and has a big appetite."

"I really want to see him up close to get a great picture of my friend Champ!" Lucy said.

Although Lucy said, "We can get a great picture," she knew *she* could get a better picture than Papa did. Lucy's mother had taught her how to use a camera.

Miss Marino gave Papa a taste. "You two came up with a winning recipe," Papa said. Lucy made Bella earn her C.C.C. ball by sitting, rolling over, and spinning.

"I need to go because I have to grade some papers," Miss Marino said. "Jerry, Lucy has her homework done so she can go with you and test the Champ, Chomp, Chum."

"We'll let you know how it goes tonight," Papa said, with a twinkle in his blue eyes. "Champ's gonna get guitar music from me, and a sunset snack courtesy of you two culinary creators."

"Lucy, be sure to wear your lifejacket," Miss Marino said.

"I will. Bye, Miss Marino," Lucy said. "Have a Champtastic night."

Chapter 19
Shocking Sight

"Use the bathroom before we go, Lucy," Papa said, as he packed some lemonade and sack lunches and loaded them in his truck. "When we're out on the boat a long time, we won't be able to do that easily."

Lucy giggled and used the bathroom in the cabin, then hopped into the truck and they drove to the lake. "Thanks for reminding me to do that, Papa," Lucy said.

"It's good to go before we're gone," Papa said, chuckling. This always struck Lucy funny how he said that. She giggled again and covered her mouth with her hand.

Lucy bounced up and down in the truck asking Papa repeatedly, "How much longer? How much longer?"

"We're almost there," Papa said.

They parked and exited the truck lickety-split.

The air smelled clean and fresh, with the scent of lilacs still blooming. Lucy and Papa walked like the wind, past the leafy trees to the lake, sending squirrels scurrying up the cedar trees along the path. Lucy noticed deer tracks heading down to the water where the deer went to drink. They looked up to the peak of Big Hollow in the distance which bordered the trail and stood proudly overlooking Bulwagga Bay.

"'I will look unto the mountain, from whence cometh my help,'" Papa said. "Today is the day, Lucy," Papa said.

Lucy & the Lake Monster

Lucy smiled. "Yes, today is our day, Papa."

A small monarch butterfly fluttered in front of them from flower to flower. Lucy and Papa heard the "crunch, crunch" sound of their footsteps walking through the woods, and the "crunch, crunch" sound of harts, hares, and hinds scurrying in the distance.

They reached and boarded their beat-up boat, with hot hopes in their hearts. The eastern cottonwood trees that grew along the shores of Lake Champlain clapped their branches in the wind.

Papa looked at the rickety rowboat and sighed. "I love this boat," Papa said. "I've had her a long, long time. Good ol' skiff."

"I love her too, Papa. Good ol' skiff. The Research Vessel is pretty special. Hey, that rhymed. Maybe that can be the next song we write." Lucy snapped her finger and sang, "The Research Vessel is pretty special..."

Papa laughed and sang along. Then, a memory returned, unbidden of his daughter, Lucy's mother. "Your Mama loved this old boat, too. I have a good memory of going out on the boat with you and your Mama when you were little."

Lucy felt a wave of grief come over her. "Heavenly Father, thank you for taking good care of Mama in Heaven," she prayed. "Calm me, Father, at this time."

She reached out to Papa and hugged him, thankful to be a family with him and sweet Bella. She would never take them for granted, knowing how precious every moment of life can be.

Lucy felt the urge to reach into her pocket to make sure Mama's alexandrite guitar pick was still there. She had taken it out of her treasure box to bring it on the boat, sensing this was a special day that required special magic.

Lucy snapped into her red lifejacket and Papa wore a blue one. She knew the routine and sat in the middle to balance the boat, so it wouldn't wobble when the waves were rough. Papa handed Lucy a snack, pushed off, and oared towards the bridge in Bulwagga Bay. They sighed with relief as they set out on the serene, fresh waters of Lake Champlain.

The shores were more crowded with onlookers that day, and the lake full of boats, because Beezel Beemish held a press conference earlier announcing she had new underwater audio equipment and that there was a good chance she and Mercenary Mike would capture Champ.

"What a beautiful night, Papa," Lucy said. He smiled warmly at her. Lucy watched the James J. Keigho tourboat tug float up the lake. It had a big letter K on the side and passengers looking out and pointing.

Lucy and Papa's favorite pastime was spending time together. Being in their boat was simply magical for them. They had both experienced happiness and tragedy, but they felt something calming about the lake, something sacred that they treasured. There was healing in the peaceful waves lapping against the boat, the oars paddling gently through the water, and the refreshing splash of water on their skin when the sun rays were hot.

Lucy looked far, then she looked to the water close by her. Lucy looked up, then she looked down to see if Champ was swimming right under her. She kept her eyes moving so she wouldn't miss Champ, as she felt the perfect breeze from the perfect evening caress her face.

There were other small crafts and ferries on the lake, but Lucy and Papa's S.S. Champfinder was the most beat-up rowboat on the glassy water. Their ancient boat explored the ancient waters of Lake Champlain.

Lucy & the Lake Monster

Lucy spotted zebra mussels on the rocks. She'd heard local fishermen talking with Papa about the multiplying mussels effecting the ecosystem of Lake Champlain. They worried the mussels and algae effected the trout population, but on this special day, the lake seemed hopeful, its water level rising high like the anticipating beat of Lucy's heart.

Papa yawned and stretched his arms to the sky. This reminded Lucy she was tired, too. He peeled a banana and gave half to Lucy to eat.

Lucy heard the swishing of the waves, then spotted something swimming in the water. "Look in that cove! A big animal swimming. Is that Champ, Papa?"

"It looks more like a deer," Papa said. Papa squinted his eyes and saw the head and huge ears. "No, bless my buttons, it's a baby moose having a leisurely swim. You don't see that every day. It probably feels good for that moose to cool off."

Lucy was in awe of the majestic moose when the cacophony of a big boat's motor interrupted her. She cringed when she saw Beezel Beemish and Mercenary Mike in their monstrous machine. It was a fifty-foot cabin cruiser, with expensive equipment like underwater fish cameras to trick Champ. The cameras looked like trout to lure him. They had an underwater drone and side scan sonars sending sound out on the starboard and port side. Beezel was proud of their high speed forward-reverse aqua-vu cameras. Mercenary Mike boasted of his big rifles to shoot and kill Champ, even though it was illegal.

Papa softly strummed his guitar. Gentle guitar music had attracted Champ before, so he wanted to try again. "It's nice being out on the lake again," Papa said. "The lake is so big and deep."

"How deep, Papa?"

152

"Over four hundred feet in its deepest part. Did you know that Lake Champlain is the sixth largest freshwater lake in our country, and it was once considered the sixth great lake?"

"Really?"

"Yes, but only for eighteen days," he said, chuckling.

"I wonder if Miss Marino knows that?"

"She might. She's pretty smart. There's a lot of lake to watch, so keep your eyes and ears open, Lucy. Be patient. I'll keep playing guitar. Do you remember when I read a passage to you from the Book of Job about the sea serpent?"

"Yes, Papa. I remember, but remind me."

"He was called the mighty sea serpent. The Leviathan. It says he has a really strong neck, and he is the fiercest creature of the sea."

"That sounds like Champ!" Lucy said, looking at Papa.

"Yes, it does," Papa said as he played quietly on his guitar again. Lucy gazed from the azure sky to the waters around her. The feeling rose up within her that Champ was closer than she thought. It was a common feeling she felt numerous times before out on the lake. It was as if he was right there with her and Papa as they enjoyed their time together in solitude, away from the world of naysayers, bullies, and grief.

Lucy gazed into the water trying to focus to see her reflection through the gentle waves. Then, from nowhere, like a kite dancing effortlessly in a warm breeze, she saw something. She shifted her gaze to the glass-smooth lake and saw a wake rolling over the crystal-clear calm surface, followed by three concentric circles of water ripples.

Lucy & the Lake Monster

All of a sudden, Lucy saw a bright flashing green light emanating from the treasured pick in her pocket. Her mother's alexandrite guitar pick was flashing like an alarm going off. This time, it wasn't police lights like at her mother's accident. She knew it was a magical message that Champ was near.

Suddenly, she saw three humps that looked like large tires sticking out of the water. "Papa, what's that?" she said. Papa was frozen in shock and didn't answer. "Papa, what's that?" Lucy repeated, pointing.

"I don't know, could it be..." Papa stammered.

Lucy whispered, "Papa, look, he's right over there!" as she pointed to his greenish-brown, turtle shell skin and humongous, thick body. Champ was the size of a school bus. "It's him, its him, ITS HIM!!" Lucy squealed.

Papa stopped picking his guitar.

Lucy remembered the Champ float they saw in town, and how she wondered if that was what Champ looked like. Now she was seeing him for real. "Get closer, Papa," she whispered. "I *know* its him this time." Champ was moving straight towards them, like a submarine gliding.

Papa lost his breath as the shock of the sight of Champ hit him. His mouth was wide open, and he could scarcely speak as he watched Champ's massive head and neck break the surface of the water. Then, Champ dipped below the glassy lake, leaving ripples, then majestically rose up again, and looked around. Then, he gracefully flipped back his horse-head, snake-like neck, and back, giving Lucy and Papa front-row seats at the performance of a lifetime.

Papa was struck with fear for a second, remembering how his daughter Lynn died looking for Champ. Then, the fear dissolved into comfort and joy at the beatific vision of Champ.

"Oh, oh, ho, ho..." Papa said, laughing. "Oh, my goodness! THERE HE IS! WOOOH! HE'S COMING THIS WAY, LUCY!"

Lucy's mouth opened wide. "This is the day I've been waiting for all my life." She felt so energized by the sight of Champ, all her tiredness was gone. She peered through her binoculars. "He's getting bigger and bigger!"

"Wow," Papa said. That's all he could say. He tried to talk and couldn't at first, seeing Champ, looking like the legends he'd heard. He angled the boat to get a better look.

Lucy noticed Champ was eating a bit of seaweed that was hanging from his mouth and he seemed hungry. She wanted to throw Champ some chum, but she didn't want to scare him away. She spoke quietly, afraid to startle him.

"I've never heard of him surfacing this long before, Papa," Lucy said quietly, not wanting to startle Champ. "Look, his tail just came out of the water."

"That's no log, that's a tail," Papa said, remembering how critics dismissed his prior pictures, calling Champ a "log." "And it's definitely not two things, like two sturgeons jumping. I've lived here all my life. I know what fish look like. It's just ONE body, the same snaky, green body we saw before. There's no doubt this time. There's no mistake on this sighting."

Champ smiled, similar to the friendly Champ statue float from the Champ Day parade. He was enjoying the sunlight that glistened off his greenish, scaly skin.

Lucy & the Lake Monster

Lucy, seeing Champ wasn't going anywhere, tossed him the Champ Chomp Chum balls.

"Here, Champy," she said as she threw him the floating C.C.C. balls. "Get it, Champ." He gobbled them with glee, coming closer and closer to the boat, following the trail of chum. "Champ's chomping the chum," Lucy said. Her face shone even more brightly than it did on Christmas morning as she giggled and squealed with excitement.

"Does he look like he did in your dream, Lucy?"

"Yes, although his tail is much longer than I thought it would be," Lucy said, mesmerized by his majestic beauty.

Papa saw Champ's head reflected in Lucy's big, blue eyes. Champ dove in the water, then came back up again. Every time Champ went underwater, Lucy was disappointed until he surfaced again, and she could see him.

"One, two, three," Lucy said, counting Champ's big humps again. It was a sight Lucy would never forget. Then, she watched his side flippers wiggle and his pointed tail wave above the water. Champ smiled, a nice, friendly smile. He didn't have scary, pointy teeth like Beezel Beemish's mean statue of him. It reaffirmed to Lucy that some people make up mean stories about others.

But Lucy had a story that wasn't made up now, right in front of her. This time, Lucy wanted to capture better evidence.

"He's so beautiful," Lucy said, savoring how the sunlight glistened off the eel-like skin of Champ's back, which glowed phosphorescent green like Mama's alexandrite guitar pick.

"Get a picture, Papa!" Lucy said.

Chapter 20
A Dream Come True

"What do I do!? Tell me again!?" Papa asked with urgency.

"Click the side button, to light up the screen, Papa! Go to the camera icon. Hurry, hurry! Click 'Photo.'"

"Photo. Okay," Papa said, pressing his phone with his fingers. "I'm gonna get it."

"Click the white button. Hurry, fast!"

"I got it, Lucy!"

"Hand it to me and I'll get a picture. In case something happens, we'll have several back-ups," Lucy said. "There he is again! I need to get another shot!"

Lucy held up Papa's camera quickly and snapped a photo. It was challenging to focus on Champ, because he wouldn't stay still. Champ was dancing everywhere, boogying on the surface of the lake.

"Got it!" she said, with a big, toothy grin. She handed the camera to Papa. "Look, Papa. How do you think it turned out?"

"Oh, I think I got Champ's body," Papa said, after looking at his blurry photo.

Lucy smiled and could hardly speak.

Lucy and Papa looked at their pictures. Both got pictures that showed Champ, and as expected, Lucy's was the best. "You

Lucy & the Lake Monster

did it, Lucy!" Papa said, his face beaming. "Wow, you got it! Yours isn't blurry like mine."

"It's definitely Champ," Lucy said.

"We got proof!" Papa said. "We're gonna show Mayor Pike and we'll get our names on that sign."

"Oh, my goodness!" She held her hands to her mouth, amazed, then waved her hands back and forth like a cheerleader. "Champ Chomp Chum really worked!"

"It sure did," Papa said. "Our name's gonna be on that sign for sure!"

She wondered if her Mama had seen and photographed Champ. She knew deep down in her knower, her Mama had captured evidence of Champ, maybe a photograph, that hadn't been discovered, yet. Maybe, it was hidden in the lake's caves. Maybe one day, her and Papa would find Mama's picture.

Lucy saw Champ in all his glory. She counted again, four sets of flippers and a tail. The ripples of Lake Champlain danced and smiled.

She extended her hand from the boat to touch Champ. She reached too far and fell headfirst into the water.

"Lucy!" her Papa called, his voice sounding muffled as she sank. She felt air hunger, fighting to breathe as she made gurgling sounds, ingesting lots of lake water in her terror. Lake Champlain was a clay-bottom lake, so it was murky and mysterious as Lucy sank down, down, down into its depths.

Beezel Beemish emerged from out of nowhere. A battalion of flies buzzed around the bowels of the lake around her boat. She seized the opportunity of the confusion to create a wake

158

then accelerate in her attempt to ram Papa's rowboat while Lucy sank. Beezel barked commands at Mercenary Mike.

"Let's capsize them just like we did before with her..." The roar of her motor accelerating drowned out the last word of her sentence. Mercenary Mike gunned their cabin cruiser and headed straight for Papa's frail skiff.

Papa was about to dive in to rescue Lucy when suddenly, Champ scooped her up. Lucy had been worried for a second when she fell in the lake. Struggling to swim, she reached in vain for something solid as she sank down, down, down.

She was surprised at how Champ was an instant lifeguard. Champ's skin was wet and cold and his back was strong and sturdy underneath her, lifting her to the surface.

The lake water in her mouth tasted like sweet medicine to Lucy now, and she knew she was in Champ's care. She rose out of the water, with life-giving breath, just like she did at her baptism. Lucy was resurrected to a new life of confidence in her faith that was now made sight, tangible and evidential.

Champ gently returned her to the boat, saving her from drowning as the town onlookers on the shore gasped. The splash doused Papa. "What a fabulous creature!" Papa said.

Papa and Lucy embraced. Champ saved her.

Papa saw Beezel and Mercenary barreling towards them in their big boat. "Save us, Champ," he said. "Swallow them up like the whale swallowed Jonah, Amen."

Champ roared at Mercenary Mike and Beezel Beemish. What Lucy and the good people saw as a miraculous manifestation of their friend Champ, was perceived differently by Mike and Beemish. They looked at the water, waves, and wake, and saw a terrible turbulence, a devilish disturbance as Champ commanded them with penetrating eyes and the breath of his nostrils to depart from Lucy and Papa, just like the Christ commanded the legion of demons to depart into the swine.

To B.B. and Mercenary, when Champ's head broke the surface of the water, his serpent neck standing six feet, he was hideous to them. They saw Champ just like the fearsome float they made of him with sharp, predatory teeth.

What Lucy saw as a beautiful mosaic of Champ's characteristics, Mercenary Mike and Beezel saw as a hair-raising, horrifying, hodgepodge of mammal, reptile, and fish, ready to eat them. To Mercenary and Beemish, Champ was formidable and ferocious, but to Lucy and Papa, Champ was gentle.

Mercenary Mike squeezed his chicken-eyes tight in terror. Champ's mighty roar echoed around him and Beemish. Mike and B.B. looked paler than death.

"Full speed ahead, Toots!" Beezel Beemish yelled like a maniac.

"Don't tell me what to do, Beemish," Mercenary Mike said, as he grabbed his .22 caliber rim-fire handgun and tried to kill Champ, but his hand was so shaky he couldn't aim. Mike, the wannabe bounty hunter, accidentally discharged his gun into their boat.

"You idiot!" Beezel screamed in her shrill voice.

Even though they'd bragged for years how they'd capture Champ, Mercenary Mike and Beezel Beemish drove away in fear, as fast as their big boat could go. The shining light of Champ's goodness pushed back their darkness, their lies that Champ was a monster to be feared.

Champ felt sad that someone would shoot at him. The sea serpent was sulky for a moment.

Mercenary Mike struggled to regain control, using the wrong amount of throttle and trim, tilting their cabin cruiser sideways. He lost his grip of the stern before straightening out and escaping the righteous anger of Champ.

"Thank you, Champy," Lucy called.

"Attaboy, Champ," Papa said raising his hands in praise.

When Champ finally appeared in all his glory, news travelled fast from locals and out-of-town campers to the four corners of the earth. Many of the people from Crown Point, Port Henry, and surrounding towns throughout the Champlain Valley and beyond saw Champ without a doubt.

"He's real. He's really, really real," baywatchers and beachgoers said to one another.

The good townspeople smiled, seeing the elusive underwater creature who lived and lurked in the lake. Miss Marino and some of Lucy's classmates saw Champ from the sandy shore. Some pointed at Champ. Others waved and smiled from their posts on the Lake Champlain Bridge. Lucy took note of this.

"Some of the people saw Champ, but I saw him first and up close," Lucy said, smiling.

They sat calmly now. Champ didn't look afraid and neither did Papa. Papa played gently on his guitar again, as he did so often and so effortlessly.

As for Lucy, when she finally saw Champ, all of him, she wasn't afraid. Champ's enchantment bathed Lucy with love and acceptance. There was a smile and spiritual connection between them. Lucy met Champ's friendly emerald eyes, sparkling and set perfectly in his plesiosaur head. Papa dried her off with a beach towel.

The C.C.C. balls brought a magical ability to communicate with Champ. Lucy talked aloud, then Champ answered telepathically. He heard her questions, then answered back. Papa could hear Lucy talking to him.

"Hi, Champ. I have some questions for you. How are you?" Lucy said. "What is it like living in the lake underwater? Is it ever lonely down there?"

An answer from Champ came in Lucy's thoughts.

I like the lake, Lucy. I have a lot of hiding places. I have family, others like me. And I've made friends with other fish.

"I'm glad you get along with the other fish," Lucy said.

I'm friends with all kinds of fish, like the great northern pike, speckled trout, large-mouthed bass, carp, and giant lake sturgeons. Even the eels try to chase me. Sometimes it's hard making friends. When smaller fish, like sunfish and minnows, see me coming, they are afraid of me and swim away. I think it's because I'm so much larger than them.

Lucy listened and nodded. "Hmm, I see," she said. "But I'm your friend, Champy."

You're my best human friend.

"I'm so glad we're best friends, Champ." Champ nodded his head so hard in agreement it raised his humpback up and down. He was so happy and playful, he twirled and chased his tail.

"Do you like the food you eat?" Lucy asked.

"That's a good question," Papa said.

Yes, especially Champ, Chomp, Chum. I like C.C.C.

"Do you hear him answer in your thoughts, Lucy?" Papa asked. "Do you know what he's saying?"

"Yeah," Lucy said, matter-of-factly. "Loud and clear. He just said he likes Champ, Chomp, Chum."

"Oh, that's nice," Papa said. "Champ likes you."

Champ answered more of her questions. He told Lucy some swimming tips so the next time she swam in the lake she could win swimming races with her friends, freckle-faced Fiona, laughing Laura, big-eyed Barb, and little Ricky Taschner.

Then, Champ whispered a secret to her. He wanted her to tell everyone in Port Henry, Crown Point, Burlington, and all the other towns surrounding Bulwagga Bay and Lake Champlain.

Take care of the lake, so it can be a good home for people, animals, and plants.

She didn't hear his voice with her ears, but heard with her heart.

Take care of where I live.

"Where do you live?" Lucy said.

I live in the shadows of Lake Champlain, but I also live in the secret place of your childlike faith.

Champ answered back by sending thought words to Lucy's brain again. Lucy took in Champ's words, then chuckled at the

163

seaweed dripping from his mouth. She threw Champ a C.C.C. ball which he devoured. Champ ate Champ Chomp Chum while Lucy ate a sandwich from her lunch bag, so Champ and Lucy shared a meal together.

One last thing. I know your mother. You're beautiful like her.

Lucy gasped. She looked Papa dead in the eyes.

"What, Lucy?" Papa asked.

Lucy paused, and smiled softly. "Champ says he knows Mama," Lucy said, full of joy.

Suddenly, Beezel startled them, driving by recklessly again, interrupting the sacred moment with her loud cabin cruiser. Ol' Skiff rocked. Lucy felt the startle and took a belly breath.

After Beezel's boat was gone, Lucy offered Champ some more Champ Chomp Chum for dessert, but he was gone. Ricky Taschner's pitching lessons that he gave Lucy on the playground paid off. She threw a long fastball with the Champ Chomp Chum. The C.C.C. balls flew through the air, full of magic and love. They drew not only Champ to return, but his offspring to the surface of Lake Champlain.

Then, Lucy saw a brownish baby Champ rise out of the water. He was only a few feet long in comparison to Daddy Champ, whose smooth, sleek body was at least twenty-five feet. Papa was right. Champ was around a long time, prehistoric, and just like people, he survived for many years by living on through his children.

"My dream has come true," Lucy said. "I've finally seen him, all of him, and his baby, too!"

"This is the third trip out on the lake we made this summer," Papa said. "There's an old saying. The third time's a charm."

Lucy smiled and played with a strand of her hair as she watched big, green Champ and his brown, smaller son glide away in the water like snakes. "Champ, since you are enchanted, and since you are a parent, I was wondering if you know my mother or my father?"

Yes, I do, Lucy because I can go places where living humans can't go while they're on earth. The place of golden streets and no defeats. The realm of magic and love.

Lucy felt her mother's spirit with her, affirming her persistence to look for Champ.

I knew if you kept looking, you'd find Champ, she heard her mother say to her heart. *Way to go, Lucy.*

She felt her mother's smiling spirit in the sun, and she felt her mother's legacy continuing on in her. She knew she'd made her Mama so proud.

Lucy threw out the rest of the food balls. "I'm making a Champ Chomp Chum trail, like Hansel and Gretel." The C.C.C. balls floated on the lake's surface, just as their Scientific Method experiment had proved. Lucy looked into the lake and addressed the fish. "All you trout and pike, don't eat the Champ, Chomp, Chum. It's only for Champ to eat!" Then she looked up and said, "That goes for you seagulls, too!"

It was the best, most exciting day of Lucy's life, and it really worked up an appetite. Lucy and Papa ate the rest of the lunches Papa packed while Champ munched on the Champ, Chomp, Chum trail. Champ and Lucy stayed near each other eating and communicating telepathically for some time.

Lucy & the Lake Monster

Lucy realized her education was more than books and classrooms and teachers like Miss Marino. She and Papa had studied the sightings and history of Champ and plesiosaurs, but now they experienced it firsthand like never before.

As they returned home in their weather-beaten boat, Lucy's soul was souring. A hole inside Papa and Lucy was temporarily filled, the grief of Lucy's mother's death abated. The hole wasn't filled completely. They would always miss her, but the sight of Champ's glorious majesty comforted them that all was well, serene like the placid lake.

Walking up the lake trail, they encountered tracks on their way home. Papa quizzed Lucy on the tracks to teach her. The first set of prints was big.

"Hmmm, well, these tracks are wide and long with claw marks," Lucy said.

"Good, Lucy," Papa said. "What else do you notice?"

"The tracks are very deep," Lucy said. "Bears like to use the prior tracks that other bears made, which makes them deeper. So...I think this is a bear track."

"Bravo," Papa said, walking further to spot some smaller tracks. "How about these footsteps?" Papa said, pointing down to tiny tracks. "I'm gonna give you a hint. Count the number of toes."

Lucy counted the toe imprints from one of the small footprints. "One, two, three, four toes."

"Now count the toes on the other foot, Lucy."

"One, two, three, four, five?" Lucy said. "That's odd. The feet are small. Is it a chipmunk, Papa?"

"No, but good guess. If it was a chipmunk, the toes would be wider apart. This is the track of one of the most plentiful animals at Lake Champlain. The gray squirrel, who has four toes on their front feet and five toes on their back feet."

Lucy looked further ahead and saw tracks with five toes on both feet. "Do you know what animal that is?" Papa asked.

Lucy held her nose shut and nodded. "P-U," she said.

Papa smiled. "You're right, a striped skunk." Papa noticed human footprints and saw the rude reporters Melnick and Kane up ahead waiting for them. "These tracks," he said, pointing at the reporters' shoe prints, "are a different type of skunk."

Lucy chuckled. "I'm tired and don't feel like talking to those reporters," Lucy said. "These two never seem to be nice."

"We're not puppets, Lucy, and they are not our puppet-masters who pull our strings and make us talk. Just because they want to do an interview with us, doesn't mean we have to. Don't let them name the time and place. We decide that."

The reporters fired questions at them rapid-fire as Lucy and Papa reached them on the path.

"How do you know it was Champ you saw? Do you have proof?" Karl Kane asked.

"Could it have been some sort of spirit or demon in human form?" Roger Melnick asked. He didn't ask this because he thought it was a possibility, he asked this to try and bait Lucy into conceding this as a possibility, so he could make her and Papa look crazy.

Lucy & the Lake Monster

"We saw Champ and got good pictures this time," Lucy said. "We're tired tonight, but we will give more details to the entire town later."

"Why later?" Melnick asked.

"What are you hiding?" Kane said.

"Anyone who wants to come out and hear us tell our first-hand account, we will have a public gathering," Papa said.

That night, Lucy and Papa slept better than they ever had before. Lucy dreamt delightful dreams of Champ, based on all she'd seen that day at Bulwagga Bay. As she dreamt of him, Champ danced in the moon, swimming in the silver light on the lake.

Chapter 21
Hometown Heroes

Lucy and Papa were shopping at Walmart, to get school clothes and groceries to make dinner. When they walked in, they passed an area in the very front of the store where all the newspapers were displayed.

Much ripple effect resulted from Lucy's brief statement to some reporters, telling them how she saw Champ. Skinny Roger Melnick and stout Karl Kane were skeptical and twisted her words, but the one decent reporter, Larry Lore, represented her fairly. She thought there was a slight chance there might be a blurb in the back of the paper.

Normally, Lucy didn't pay much attention to newspapers because she found many of the stories were bad news or boring. But when she glanced at the newsstand, she recognized a familiar face....HER!

"Look!" Lucy said. "That's me!"

"Whaa...oh my...." Papa said, barely able to speak for a second. "Lucy...that's you!"

"That *is* me," Lucy said, picking the newspaper up and looking at her giant, color, front-page photo.

"You made the front page of the newspapers!" Papa said.

"That is so cool," Lucy said.

Lucy became a star, a media darling talking about Champ, with newspaper headlines like:

Lucy & the Lake Monster

YOUNG GIRL BRINGS RENEWED INTEREST TO CHAMP
LUCY LAGO AND THE LAKE MONSTER
CHAMP RETURNS! LUCY AND JERRY LAGO'S CHAMP PICS
LUCY SEES THE LAKE MONSTER

Lucy thought about a story she'd heard in Sunday School about a young boy named David who beat a giant named Goliath in a fight. Here she was, just nine years old, and many bigger people had tried to find Champ and make money off him, like Mercenary Mike and Beezel Beemish. Yet, little Lucy is the one that ends up on the front-page of every newspaper, with the byline by Larry Lore, the most respected journalist in the Lake Champlain region.

Lucy was front-page news and as Port Henry's newest celebrity, the town gathered to honor her and Papa. A crowd welcomed Papa and Lucy on Champ Day as heroes, the guests of honor. A Champ tee-shirt with an image of Lucy seeing Champ, and Champ reflected in her eyes caught on as the latest fashion fad. Many in the crowd were wearing it. Most of the townspeople were nice, but a few reporters and scientists were still skeptical. Children from all over the world sent video messages telling Lucy and Papa they believed in Champ and believed in them.

Mayor Pike, a short, roly-poly man, unveiled two signs with Lucy and Papa's names on them, written in gold letters. The Bulwagga Bay Champ eyewitness sign added their names for their Champ sightings, and Stewart's Ice Cream added their names to a sign for finishing the Champ Monster Banana Split at Lucy's birthday party.

Then, in an unexpected surprise, Mayor Pike unveiled a part of the sign that had her mother's name, too.

"Lynn Lago saw Champ many times and told me her testimony," Mayor Pike said. "The Board of Trustees of the Port Henry Chamber of Commerce has included her name, her father's, and her daughter's."

Lucy stared again and again at their names in gold letters on the sign:

LUCY LAGO
JERRY LAGO
LYNN LAGO

Lucy knew there was a big difference between her and all the other eyewitness names on the Bulwagga Bay sign. Champ had stayed above water longer for her than for any of the other three hundred witnesses. Papa had been around Lake Champlain for decades, and he knew many of the people whose names were on the sign. He had heard their stories of how Champ would show himself, then disappear in the blink of an eye. They got a quick glimpse, but Lucy and Papa saw Champ the longest.

The Port Henry High School band played on the bandstand attached to the raised platform. During mealtime, served outside by Lake Champlain, Ricky Taschner approached Lucy and grinned.

"Can I have your autograph?" Ricky said to Lucy. Lucy laughed and signed her autograph. Many people mobbed Lucy. Her friends from school kept saying "Wow, Lucy, wow!"

Lucy and Papa were eating Annie's Michigan Dogs, the best michigans in the North Country when Butch the Bully came up to Lucy. His face bowed low in shame, and he stared at the ground. "I was wrong," Butch said softly. "You saw Champ. I'm sorry," he said, lifting his head and entering a state of grace. The front-page articles and Lucy's Champ photos even made a believer out of Butch.

Lucy & the Lake Monster

"I'm sorry too," Mousey McFarland, Butch's short shadowy companion echoed. He was standing behind big Butch, partially hidden by Butch's bulk. Mousey's voice was a little less weaselly than usual.

"If anyone messes with you in the future, let me know," Butch said. "And they'll have to answer to me."

"Thank you. I accept both of your apologies," Lucy said to Butch and Mousey. The two boys walked away. Lucy thought she even saw a tear in Butch's eye.

He went from Butch the Bully to Butch the Believer, Lucy thought to herself, as she considered Butch's come-to-Jesus moment. She looked at Papa and he nodded knowingly at her and winked.

Lucy realized it wasn't just the bullies who changed. She changed, too. For so long, she saw herself and Papa as the underdogs, in their makeshift cabin and beat-up boat. They were outsiders, mocked by the "normies" as she sometimes called the "normal" people who snickered and whispered about her and Papa behind their backs, calling them "crazy" for seeking Champ.

With the town's shift in attitude, and Lucy and Papa going from mocked eccentrics to front-page news, Lucy gained a confidence that she wasn't an outsider anymore. She was part of her community now. With this shift, she found she no longer needed the approval of anyone else. She liked the applause, but she didn't need it.

Lucy spotted Miss Marino and invited her to sit with her and Papa. "Look at the picture of Champ I took," Lucy said, pointing to her photo. "See, Champ's head is right there."

"That's better than the Mansi photo," Miss Marino said. "Your viewpoint is much closer than Sandra Mansi's was. This is gonna

172

be the new shot of the twenty-first century that's heard around the world," Miss Marino said as she winked at Lucy. She laughed, beaming with pride over Lucy's accomplishment. "You're so famous I've seen it in the newspapers and heard it on television."

Lucy clapped with excitement, overwhelmed to see her mother's name on the sign with hers and Papa. She wasn't just clapping for herself becoming famous, but for her Mama, Papa, and Champ, as well. Her dream of seeing Champ came true, exceedingly and abundantly above and beyond all she had hoped for. It was beyond words, ineffable, beyond any concept of lake monsters and plesiosaurs.

Some scientists and reporters hovered around Papa and Lucy like vultures with questions, so Mayor Pike stood up to moderate. He guided Papa and Lucy to their seats on the bandstand, then approached a microphone that sat on the raised platform.

"As mayor of our fair city of Port Henry, I welcome you all. I don't have to tell any of you that there's an awful lot of buzz going around this town, and these two honored guests, Jerry Lago and his granddaughter Lucy, are the subject of the scuttlebutt."

"Way to go, Lucy," Ricky Taschner cried out from the middle of the crowd, his voice projecting through the toothless gap in his grin. Lucy's other best friends, freckle-faced Fiona, big-eyed Barb, and laughing Laura gave her thumbs-ups.

"These two are front page news, the biggest celebrities in Port Henry right now," Mayor Pike continued. "Jerry and his granddaughter, little Lucy, have a couple pictures of Champ and are the eyewitnesses to the best sighting of Champ ever." Mayor Pike turned to look at Lucy directly. "I'm really proud of you two. You've brought so much revenue and nationwide attention to the Lake Champlain region. Champ tee-shirts are selling like hotcakes worldwide. Souvenirs and tours are at an all-time high. I want to thank you both for bringing so much positive attention to our friend Champ, and putting him on the radar, more than he ever has been before. Thank you, Lucy and Jerry Lago for putting Bulwagga Bay on the map. For decades, our most famous hometown hero was Johnny Podres, the great left-handed pitcher for the Dodgers. But now, joining him at the top of the list is Lucy Lago and Champ. Thank you, Lucy."

"You're welcome, Mister Mayor," Lucy said, brushing her hair back with her hand as the crowd roared with cheers and applause.

"Our pleasure, Mayor Pike," Papa said. "You can thank Lucy for those photos, hers turned out better than mine. She's so good at taking pictures and writing stories, maybe one day some of you reporters will be working for Lucy." He chuckled and grinned at reporters Karl Kane and Roger Melnick.

"There are scientists here, there are reporters here, there are many luminaries of our townspeople here, so I want to give you all a chance to ask some questions. Then, I want to give Jerry and Lucy the final word on Champ," Mayor Pike said.

Sam the skeptical scientist walked up to Lucy, his head bowed forward a bit. "Lucy, you've made me think of a side of life that I am skeptical about. You made me ask myself if I have a closed mind and if I am blind to certain things."

"I'm glad, Professor," Lucy said.

"I still don't know how Champ, if he exists, survived the Ice Age and would end up in a lake rather than the ocean," Sam said.

Lucy pondered, gathering her thoughts. "I believe that a long time ago, the saltwater sea was connected to the lake," Lucy said.

174

"Champ could've come from the sea to the lake, and adapted to his new freshwater environment over time. Adaptation is a primary concept in science."

Scientist Sam was surprised Lucy used big adult words like "adaptation" and "concept." Lucy remembered Papa told her "Leaders are readers," so she had been reading all the science books she could.

Reporter Larry Lore interviewed Lucy. "Champ is America's Loch Ness," Lore said, referencing the monster in the Highlands of Scotland.

"No!" Lucy said, interrupting him. Just then, the memory came back of what Mama had told her. "I think Scotland should call Nessie Scotland's Lake Champlain Monster," Lucy said with a smile. "It's Champ's turn to get the recognition he deserves."

"How long was the sea serpent?" Lore asked as a follow-up question.

"About the length of a schoolbus," Lucy said.

"Color?" Lore asked.

"He was different shades of green," Lucy said. "The baby Champ was brownish."

Lindsay Brookens, a female reporter who was tall with brunette hair approached Lucy. "What did you feed Champ?"

"He loves our Champ Chomp Chum, a delicious combination of peanut butter, veggies, honey, and marshmallow crème rolled in balls," Lucy said.

"What kind of vegetables?" Lindsay Brookens asked.

Lucy & the Lake Monster

"Celery, corn, carrots, lettuce, and spinach," Lucy said. "I ate lunch with Champ. I ate my sandwich while he ate Champ, Chomp, Chum. And I took a picture to prove it."

"We'll have to authenticate that picture. Just because people believe a legend doesn't make it real," reporter Karl Kane said to Papa.

"But then again, just because you can't see something, doesn't mean it isn't real," Papa said.

"But why can't we see it more? With all the cellphone cameras and three hundred supposed eyewitnesses, why don't we have better pictures or videos to see Champ?" Kane asked.

"Champ is like any animal," Lucy said. "Animals don't want to show themselves if people are watching with a camera. They don't feel safe. Champ's real. Trust me on that."

"Lucy and I saw Champ clear as day this last time," Papa said. "I admit, I didn't get a good picture, because I was really excited to see him. It was a moment of awe, but my picture this time is a lot better. It's blurry, but not as blurry as last time. Lucy's picture's far better. You can clearly see Champ's head."

"How convenient," reporter Roger Melnick scoffed. "You see the sea monster finally for over five minutes and all you get is a couple mediocre pictures?

"As mayor of this town, I want everyone to keep their questions respectful," Mayor Pike said. "That goes for you Roger Melnick and your 'gotcha journalism.'"

"It's okay, Mayor," Papa said. "People need lots of stretching room for their feelings and questions. My pictures aren't perfect, but at least we saw him real good this last time. People with faith in their hearts will believe us."

"Yeah," Lucy said. "They do. I know, and Papa knows, we saw Champ this time."

Lucy held up her pictures which were a little clearer than Papa's, but Beezel Beemish had spread a lie in the press that Lucy's pictures were photoshopped and fake.

"With all the cellphones around now, why don't we have even better pictures that prove it beyond a reasonable doubt?" reporter Roger Melnick asked.

"Most people on the lake aren't looking," Lucy said. "They're out fishing and swimming. Most people aren't looking with a camera in their hand."

"And when Champ surfaces, it's often just momentarily," Papa said. "People aren't ready to take a picture in the spur-of-the-moment. And the lake's awfully big."

"Let me ask you a question, Mister Melnick," Lucy said. "Have you ever seen a car accident?"

"Of course," Melnick said.

"Show me a picture you took of the accident happening."

"I don't have one," Melnick answered.

"Why not? If the car wreck is real, why aren't there more pictures of the thousands of wrecks that are happening?"

"Because they happen so fast and everyone is in shock so that, in those fleeting few seconds, no one thinks to get a pic-..." Melnick stopped speaking, mid-sentence, realizing Lucy outsmarted him and made her point.

Lucy & the Lake Monster

"Exactly. Champ appears for a few seconds, once in a while, and the witnesses are in awe. But we're gonna keep looking until we get an even greater picture," Lucy said. "But we believed in Champ in our hearts, even before we saw him."

"The things you can see are temporal. The things you don't see are eternal," Papa said.

"Like what?" reporter Karl Kane asked.

Lucy grinned and chimed in. "Like Love. Spirit. Magic," Lucy said, remembering Papa's answer to Sam the Scientist at their last press conference.

"Attagirl, Lucy," Ricky Taschner said.

Papa touched Lucy's head affectionately. "Some say, 'Let me see first, then I'll believe.' Lucy believed first, so she saw," Papa said.

"That's okay for a child," Kane said. "They believe in Champ, and Santa, and unicorns. Lucy lives in make-believe."

"I know that Champ is real!" Lucy said.

Papa paused, then answered. "A wise man said two thousand years ago, 'Unless you become like a little child, you cannot see.' Maybe only those who really believe can see him. Champ got close to Lucy and stayed near her. He cares about her in a way he never cared for a person before, the way he surfaced and stayed by her for a much longer time than ever before."

"All you have are stories," Kane said.

"Stories are awfully powerful things," Papa said. "They helped Lucy and me through the sad times."

"You want me to believe based on the word of a nine year-old girl?" Melnick asked.

Papa scratched his salt and pepper beard and remembered a quote from his favorite teacher. "Whoever receives one child such as this in My name, receives Me; and whoever receives Me, receives not Me but the One who sent Me," Papa said.

Chapter 22
Magic and Love

Papa put his hand on Lucy's shoulder. "I'm proud of you, Lucy. I'm proud of your imagination. And your faith. And your heart. I'm amazed."

Mayor Pike approached the mike again. "I must say I'm amazed as well at this young girl's intellect and how Lucy's findings match the findings of all the best eyewitness accounts. On that wonderful note, I want to give Jerry and Lucy the last word, to share anything about what they saw regarding Champ, and what they thought and felt. Maybe something they learned. Jerry you go first, then Lucy."

Papa rubbed his beard and walked to the mike. He was a humble man without experience in public speaking. He spoke from the heart, which is always the most powerful speech of all, much better than reading a prewritten speech.

"All my life, I heard of people looking for Champ," Papa said. "I believe in my heart I'd seen him long ago, but it was quick. Lucy and I went out time after time, because it was her late mother's dream to see Champ. Her mother was my daughter, Lynn. When we finally saw him, it wasn't for just a moment, but for a good while. I learned that when you truly believe in something, you don't want to quit. You keep looking and looking. You strive to reach the goal of your dream."

"We're proud of you, Jerry," Miss Marino yelled from the crowd.

Lucy & the Lake Monster

"Thank you, Miss Marino," Papa said, waving at her and thinking how lovely she looked in her vintage violet bohemian dress. "Hopefully, it won't be our last time," Papa said, looking at Lucy. "Right, Lucy?"

"Right," Lucy replied.

Lucy spotted Mister Brook, the tipsy man from Captain Blye's and he was smiling and sober, in his right mind. She remembered praying for him before her lunch that day and realized another prayer was answered. Lucy whispered a prayer of thanks in her heart.

"What do you have to say, Lucy?" Papa asked.

"I agree with Papa. I believe in Champ, that he is real. It was my dream and I followed it and I encourage all of you to follow your dreams, it's what makes you happy. If you haven't reached your dream, keep working on it."

"Amen," the reporter Larry Lore said, who made Lucy a household name.

"Bravo," the nasty reporter Melnick said. Lucy was shocked.

"Yay, Lucy," Kane, the other cruel reporter said. Lucy did a double take.

Lucy was surprised both bad-behaving reporters smiled and applauded her, along with the skeptical scientist Sam. She realized for a brief moment, they were all sorry for their past treatment of her. All were reconciled and at peace. Champ had restored the town and made them all one. It was as if every knee bowed and every tongue confessed that Champ was real. Lucy glanced to Lake Champlain. The water was soothing and still.

The normies are no better than me, and I'm no better than them, Lucy thought to herself. This thought felt like a homecoming to her.

Lucy had only one lingering bad thought, a discerning of spirits. The mystique and magic of Lake Champlain brought a revelation to her mind. She wondered if Beezel Beemish and her boyfriend were somehow responsible for her mother's accident. She couldn't shake the feeling that they rammed into her boat, just as they tried to do to her and Papa.

Maybe if Mama's missing camera is found, it will have a clue to the mystery. Pursuing that will have to wait for another day, Lucy thought. *Today is a day to celebrate.*

Lucy looked at the scientists and realized they were no longer her enemies, even though Sam had been quite rough in his past questions. The skeptics and scientists were her teachers, too. They motivated her to study more about plesiosaurs and the history of Champ sightings. She had so much more knowledge of biology, history, science, and zoology than when she started her adventures.

Lucy turned her eyes from the reporters and scientists to the growing crowd. She stood in front of the cheering townspeople on Champ Day and spoke in her loud, outside voice, sharing the secret message Champ gave her.

"When I saw Champ, I threw him some food," Lucy said. "A concoction we call Champ Chomp Chum. When I threw the food balls, Champ danced on the water, waving his fins."

"Was he halfway in the water, dancing with his head and body, or walking on water with his entire body?" Larry Lore asked.

Lucy & the Lake Monster

"Champ was walking on water like the miracle in Bible days," Lucy said. "It was like something out of a cartoon. He was having fun, dancing with his entire body."

"Ladies and gentlemen, no one has ever seen Champ's entire body," Mayor Pike said. "There are sketches of parts of Champ's body from the man who discovered the lake, Samuel de Champlain. But no one has ever seen *all* of Champ, until Lucy. Lucy Lago will go down in history, for seeing Champ's entire body dancing on the water."

"Animals and nature have a special dance. We all have to live together, people, plants, and animals as one community. Pollution is harmful to lake loons and other water fowl, fish, and even to us," Lucy continued. "It stops the music and the rhythm of the dance. Champ wants us to take better care of the lake, to be a good home for future generations. If we do this, we are in Champ's camp! Who is gonna join me and camp with Champ?"

The crowd cheered, in support of Lucy's words.

Then Lucy read a little poem she had written:

> *Champ is not just an animal*
> *Or a monster to fear*
> *He's a fellow divine creature*
> *And his home is right here*
> *This is where I want him to be*
> *Forever our friend, forever free*

Then, Papa strummed his guitar and sang new lyrics with Lucy about their adventures:

> *Lucy saw Champ floating on the sea.*
> *But her neighbors said, "It's just an old tree."*
> *The town grew quiet and looked at Lucy.*
> *She said, "You only believe in what you can see."*

184

Then, Lucy looked to the lake, then she looked above.
And said, "The best things you can't see, like Magic and Love..."

Lucy waved goodbye to the cheering crowd. "Thank you, everyone! Have a Champtastic day!" Lucy said.

"I'm so proud of you, Lucy," her teacher Miss Marino said, with her frizzy hair blowing in the warm wind.

Papa and Lucy felt proud of all they accomplished together. Their fear and pain from Lynn Lago's accident was healed in their beatific vision of Champ. It transformed them, replacing fear with faith. Their heart wounds were healed and were now scars, memories of Lynn that no longer haunted them.

Papa and Lucy took their Research Vessel out on the lake again, for a relaxing joyride to celebrate. They oared out to the depths of the lake on their rickety rowboat.

"You sure are the best granddaughter I could ever have. You're such a gift from God to me, Lucy. I'm so happy that we got to see Champ and many more people believe us." His face radiated the warmth of a fireplace on Christmas day.

"Me too, Papa."

Questions popped up in Lucy's mind like bread popping out of a toaster.

Will I see Champ again? Will I find out what happened to my mother? she thought.

Papa thought to himself too, hoping against hope his daughter, Lynn, was still alive. He had more questions he thought about.

Lucy & the Lake Monster

Is it possible the mystery of Lynn's boating accident and disappearance will ever be solved? Papa thought. *Is it even possible she could still be...*

As Lucy, Bella, and Papa paddled the S.S. Champfinder (aka Research Vessel) toward their humble cabin, a still, small voice inside Papa assured him they would find the answers in their next journey. The lake was pure and peaceful again to Papa Jerry and Lucy. The best was yet to come.

"When I close my eyes, I will see Mama and Champ again, because they are always with me," Lucy said. Lucy trusted her heart more than anything anybody else could ever say.

"'Faith is the substance of things hoped for, the evidence of things not seen,'" Papa said. "'If you only believe, all things are possible to the one who believes.'"

"It's the magic of believing," Lucy said, as she often did. Bella barked a hearty "Amen."

Just then, Champ poked out his "chicken nugget-shaped turtle head," as Lucy called it. He rose from Lake Champlain and smiled at little Lucy. She smiled and waved back. Champ submerged back under the water.

Lucy looked out at Bulwagga Bay. She surveyed the shore and marvelled at the majestic cedar, birch, and oak trees sprouting up the shoreline. She thought about what she'd learned on her Champtastic journey. She repeated some lyrics to herself she'd written with Papa. They said what her and Papa believed, and what all wonderful people believe:

I look to the lake and I look above
The best things you can't see, like Magic and Love
Magic and Love
Magic and Love...

Richard Rossi & Kelly Tabor

THE END

About
The Authors

Kelly Tabor is a retired fourth-grade school teacher. She regaled her students for thirty-two years with stories of her childhood adventures, searching for the mysterious creature that lurks in the murky waters of Lake Champlain. *Lucy and the Lake Monster* is her debut novel.

Richard Rossi is an Academy Award considered filmmaker and multi-medium artist. *Lucy and the Lake Monster* is his third published novel.

Lucy & the Lake Monster

Also by Richard Rossi

Books

Canaan Land

Stick Man: The Long Awaited Coming-of-Age Novel

Sister Aimee: The Aimee Semple McPherson Story

Create Your Life: Daily Meditations On Creativity

Films

Canaan Land

Baseball's Last Hero: 21 Clemente Stories

Sister Aimee: The Aimee Semple McPherson Story

Saving Sister Aimee

Live At Graffiti's

Quest for Truth

For more information on Richard Rossi's music, movies, books, and art, visit: richardrossistore.com

Made in United States
North Haven, CT
20 July 2022

21589369R00109